MW01223396

"Tony's Joe"

Just an Average Joe

Volume 1

The Beginning

First printed 2018

ISBN – 13: 978-1984190444
ISBN – 10: 198419044x

This novel is a Biographical / Fiction work. It is a collection of stories and facts loosely based on my life. Taking literary advantage to create a more memorable experience for the readers. I may have changed some identifying characteristics and names maintain their anonymity in some instances.

Original illustrations/ Photographs by Joseph A Agostino, unless otherwise noted in photograph captions.

Email: joeagostino@outlook.com

Phone: 306 640 2415

Published by CreateSpace Independent Publishing Platform

Printed by CreateSpace Print on Demand Services in USA

This work is dedicated to Nickys Joe for all his help on the history portion of the story and Bev for all her support and understanding, and countless hours of proofing, and all of those who impacted my life, from a gleam in dads eye to a married man.

Thank You
"Tony's Joe"

Prologue

It was a chilly night as I made my way to bed. Bev was already sleeping and before long, my eyes closed and my brain and body were very relaxed. It was 3:00 AM, when my eyes popped open from a dead sleep, thoughts were running through my head, like a river running to the ocean. What am I going to do now, retirement has struck like a five-pound hammer hitting a nail with the force of a hurricane. I sat up, legs dangling over the edge of the bed, stories and thoughts started to flow through my head, happy, sad and funny just a mix mash of everything, life flashing before my eyes. I laid back down tried to go back to sleep, and before I could enter that blissful state of hibernation for the second time, I thought you have had a good life, years full of happiness, tears, and adventures.

I woke early and realized I was heading to my 67th year. Grabbed a coffee, sat down and cleared the cobwebs from my brain. Thinking, I should put some of my thoughts down on paper, before age makes them fade into oblivion. Why would one enter such a daunting task, keep the history and stories alive, more for my kids, relatives, and friends than anything else?

As a result, "Tony's Joe" Just an Average Joe came to be.

"Tony's Joe" was a nickname that was used throughout my childhood. It was used to distinguish me from my other cousins at the time, Raymond's Joe and Nicks Joe.

Volume 1 covers a period when my Grandparents immigrated to Canada, my parents met and were married, I was born, and then got married in November 1971. It is a collection of stories and facts loosely based on my life. Taking literary advantage to create a more memorable experience for the readers.

Volumes two and three will continue with my life from November 1971 onward.

"Tony's Joe" Just an Average Joe is a story of a man's ventures that start's with some family history. My story starts in Italy and Sweden with my grandparents, finally to the Twin Cities, Fort William, and Port Arthur, Ontario on the head of Lake Superior. It chronicles Joe's early life as he grew up in and around Port Arthur and Fort William, now known as Thunder Bay. Life experiences, travel's and adventures are told through different tales, from my memories and the memories, of people, I have met and touched over the years.

TABLE OF CONTENTS

TABLE OF CONTENTS

TABLE OF CONTENTS

Part 1
Origins

New Beginnings - Italy

The story starts in Mammola, Italy in 1882 when Giuseppe (Joseph) Agostino my grandfather was born, fondly known as Papu. The area, well known for its Greek history. Inhabited since the time of Ancient Greece, its origins date back to the IV - V century BC, hence the Greek overtures in my Grandpa's name. Mammola, situated between the Aspromonte and Serre mountains prime habitat for porcini mushrooms, olives and the manufacture of olive oils. Lush green countryside and a temperature range of 8 degrees Celsius in the winter to averages of 30 degrees Celsius in the summer. A beautiful place to grow up steeped in history and the love of life. Papu was born with a clubfoot and as a result, had a definite limp. He grew up in the countryside around Mammola finding work when he could.

Angela Maria Agostino was born in Mammola, March 7, 1886, fondly known as Nana. Both she and papu had the same surname, but blood did not relate them.
They meet sometime before 1902, and a beautiful romance for the ages came to be. On November 27, 1902, Nana and Papu married in a simple ceremony by the standards of the day but created a joining that would last a lifetime.

Papu was a laborer and times were terrible at this stage of his life. A qualified worker like a carpenter, in Italy, could earn up to $9.00 for a 56-hour workweek.

From 1902 to 1909 Papu and Nana had a wonderful simple life in Mammola with family and friends although they were living through poor

[2]

economic times, they were happy even though they had many sad moments. It's said, that they had four children, but there are only records of three. The three children were Rosa Maria, Nicodemo (Nicola), and Francesco.

The children died in and around Mammola. Rosa Maria, at three months, Nicodemo (Nicola) passed away when he was three years old. Francesco, it was said possessed a gift from God departed at the age of seven years. With the loss of their children, this must have placed a terrible strain on their relationship, but I am sure their faith helped them through this challenging time. By 1908, Papu must have thought to himself that there had to be a better place for him and his family. He was living through a period in Italy that had weak economic conditions and an even more unfortunate political climate, a climate where the government of the day repressed political views that would be a benefit to the average family. On December 28, 1908, an earthquake with a magnitude of 7.1 virtually destroyed Reggio Calabria area. The district around Messina some 90 kilometers away, had been flattened. I am sure that this might have been the last straw for Papu as he decided to immigrate to North America.

As I mentioned before, Italians came to North America to escape political policies and economic hardships. Between 1900 and 1913, over 3 million Italians immigrated to North America. Many Italians wanted to acquire land in Italy, but it was out of reach. Many Italians moved to America to work and earn money, then repatriate back to Italy.

The Canadian government at this period did not actively encourage Italian immigrants to come to Canada. They thought they would not make superb farmers or pioneers, and were ill-suited to the pioneering lifestyle.

Papu took the decision to leave his family and immigrate to North America when he was 26 years old. He had heard that a good worker could earn up to $18 for a 56-hour workweek, more than double what he was making now. He made his way to Naples. He purchased a ticket, boarded the ship *Europa* and traveled to the United States. The ship docked at New York, New York, on February 1, 1909. He listed his wife, Angela Maria, as his departure contact while his destination was Syracuse, New York. While in Syracuse, he stayed with his friend Giuseppe Nicodemo.

Papu had heard that in Canada, the railway companies required a constant supply of labor for construction and maintenance on the tracks and equipment, as well there was work in mining camps with different mining companies. So in December 1909, Giuseppe Agostino (Papu) entered Canada at the Port of Niagara Falls, New York and listed his destination as Fort William, Ontario (Thunder Bay South). When he arrived, he moved to Port Arthur (Thunder Bay North) and got a job working as a laborer for the Canadian National Railway (CNR).

It took a few years, but finally, Angela Maria (Nana) got word to come to Canada. Nana immigrated to Canada (via the United States) on April 17, 1913, when she was 27 years of age. Nana was finally on her way to meet her soul mate and leave the happiness and sadness in Mammola behind. Nana and her brother Domenico traveled on the ship *Konig Albert* that departed Naples/Genoa, Italy and docked at New York, New York. She listed her occupation as a housewife and her religious denomination, Catholic.

[4]

Her destination, Fort William, Ontario, Canada, (Thunder Bay South), her departure contact was her mother, Rosa Maria Vigliarolo, in Mammola, Reggio Calabria, Italy. I do not think that Papu and Nana ever made it back to Italy so that when they left, it was likely the last time they ever saw their parents. Nana finally arrived in Thunder Bay North into the arms of her soul mate Giuseppe (Papu) to start a new life in a world that offered prosperity and hope.

New Beginnings – Sweden

Meanwhile, in Sweden, Granma and Grandpa's life was getting underway.

Alford Bernhard Johansson, (Grandpa), born April 23, 1897, in the Norrbotten Region of Sweden. Grandpa grew up in this area. He worked wherever he could. Doing whatever jobs he could find, farming, logging, at this time he started learning a new trade as a carpenter.

Estrid Linna Bergstrom (Grandma) was born on October 6, 1902, in a small town called Alvsby, Norrbotten. About 100 kilometers away from where grandpa was born. They both probably lived a relatively simple life, which was prevalent at the time. The areas they lived in offered farming, logging, and other sorts of work that was required to sustain small towns at the time. The land in which they grew up would have been somewhat similar to the Thunder Bay area. Even though life was simple at the time, many Swedish people were immigrating to other lands because of economic, religious, and political reasons.

Grandma and grandpa met in 1922. They married in 1923 and had one daughter who was born in Sweden, Aunty Barbro.

Shortly after they were married, grandpa was in touch with his brother Carl, in Thunder Bay South (Fort William), Ontario and the decision was to leave Sweden and head for North America. Grandpa left Goteborg, Sweden on November 24, 1923, traveled to England then on to North America aboard a ship called the *Montcalm*. In December 1923, Grandpa after a couple of weeks on the ocean, arrived in St

John, New Brunswick. According to his declaration of passage to Canada, his preferred occupation was farming and his intended profession, he would work at anything. His fare third class paid for by his brother Carl was around $200 the equivalent of $2800 today. He made his way to Thunder Bay South (Fort William) Ontario to his brother's house at 343 N Harold Street, roughly traveled 2500 kilometers. He started this journey with $50 in his pocket.

Once grandpa started working, he got word back to grandma and sent her the third class fares required for her and Aunty Barbro. Grandma with a little one in tow, who was under one year old, started a new adventure. They made their way to the port, boarded the SS. Drottningholm, and departed on May 24, 1924, from Göteborg, Sweden as they set off to their new destination in Canada. They landed in Halifax, Nova Scotia about 2 to 3 weeks later. Once they cleared customs, grandma told them that her final goal was to reach Thunder Bay South (Fort William), Ontario to join her husband and start their new life together in the modern world. She had $25 in her pocket. Grandma and Grandpa's surname was changed to Johnson from Johansson when they landed in Canada. Aunty Barbro became Aunty Barbara. They started their new adventure at 343 N Harold Street.

Typical Passengers ships of the time

S.S. KONIG ALBERT, 1899 North German Lloyd
Courtesy The Peabody Museum of Salem

This card, posted in Göteborg, February 2, 1924, to Miss Hildur Karlsson, Stockholm.

The SS. Drottningholm built in 1904, then purchased by the SAL (Swedish American Line) in 1920. The ship then, sold in 1948 and scrapped in 1955. During the time the vessel belonged to SAL, it carried more than 220,000 passengers.

A New Life in a New World

By 1913, Papu and Nana Agostino had started their adventures in Canada and 1924; Grandpa and Grandma joined together again. They were ready to begin their unique experience's in the modern world.

Both couples, now situated in Canada, far away from their homelands, I am sure that they both endured hardships to get to the new world and new dreams. They traveled long distances to get to ports so they could depart on the ships to start their adventures. Going across the ocean would have been a daunting task in itself. Then after two to three weeks in third class steerage or less, they would have arrived at different ports, only to embark on another journey to get to their final destinations.

How Papu and Nana got to the U.S.A. and Canadian border remains a mystery, but chances are the railway had something to do with it. Grandpa and Grandma in all probability took the rails to get from the east coast to Thunder Bay. Both sets of grandparents once landed had another three to four thousand kilometers to get to their final destination. Travel by rail in the early part of the century was not a picnic either. In The Pier 21 Story by J.P. LeBlanc, he described these immigrant trains as follows:

Immigrant Travel

"The immigrant trains on tracks adjacent to the Southend station in the 1920's, were called colonist trains and were primitive in nature. Coal burning stoves at each end of the cars provided heat, and the dining facilities left much to be desired." Many immigrants, military service personnel, displaced people used these trains to get to their final destinations.

As I sit and write, thoughts cross my mind, what did they think about on this journey. Where they romantic travels or just uncomfortable excursions or a little of both. A Dutch immigrant, Th. J. Duiverman never forgot his train trip. His comments were:

Outside Pier 21, in 1920, to get to our train we had to walk over cinders and railroad tracks. With wooden benches, no sleeping cars and lack of food the train trip was long and arduous. You had buy food before you left Halifax. Otherwise, it could be a long hungry trip. The trains at the time were steam driven and were dirty, and everyone was filthy. The lighting systems were not very good and left the passengers at night entirely in the dark.

An Italian immigrant Serverino Andolfatto recalls:
"The coach of the train was frigid and had uncomfortable wooden benches, but Serverino did not care. Now he sat with new friends that he had made on the ship. The traveling companions were fascinated by the new land, the ever-changing beautiful landscape going by outside the train windows."

Many immigrants, lured by the advertisements of the two big railway companies in Canada. They heard stories that promised a prosperous future, but the promises proved empty for some while they worked long hours on the farms, in the bush and on the railways for low wages. My ancestors made the most of it and provided their families with a good start in the new world, leaving heartaches, and family thousands of miles away.

Archive photo from www.pier21.ca, a new boatload of new Canadians embarking on the rest of their journey.

Nana and Papu Early Life

Nana and Papu settled into a cozy life in Little Italy and owned a little place on Machar Avenue as well as a small grocery store on Bay Street.

The 1921 census showed that they had three boarders living with them as well as their children. At the time, Papu was earning more than $800 annually, very different from his $200 per year in Italy. He owned his home; as well, he retained a small business. When Nana arrived in 1913, it did not take them long to start a new family.

Family picture late 1920's dad looks like he is 3 or 4 years old. Nana has her hand on my Dad's shoulder

Dad had a large family, the dates of their births are as follows:

- Aunty Carmela (Carmel) Born 1914
- Aunty Rosa Maria (Rosie) 1915
- Uncle Franceso (Frank) 1917
- Uncle Vincenzo (Jimmy) 1918
- Uncle Giovanni (John) 1919
- Aunty Ida (Edith) 1921
- Uncle Nicholas (Nick) 1923
- My Dad Antonio (Tony) 1924
- My Godfather Uncle Raymondo (Raymond) 1926.

Sometime after 1921, Papu and Nana moved to 50 Ontario Street, and they open a small grocery store on the corner of Ontario and Cornwall Streets in Little Italy. It was a remarkable place to grow up as everyone took care of each other.

The family was growing, and Papu was able to provide a decent living for his family. The family was growing up in Little Italy, and I am sure all the kids were attending school at least some of the time. They would have been attending St. Joseph's school on the corner of Ontario and John Street.

50 Ontario Street Papu and Nana's Home

*Imagine the sidewalk filled with produce. That is
what I remember growing up.*

In 1915, a young fellow named Arthur Squitti was born on Secord Street not very far from Papu and Nana's house. A tragedy happened in 1919. Arthur's mother passed away leaving him without a loving mother when he was four years old. You could run into this young fellow selling newspapers on the street corner. Nana treated Arthur's like one of her own children, Arthur hung around the store on Ontario Street, and he considered Nana as his mother. Nana became a source of much of Art's loving personality. Arthur became a commercial fisherman on Lake Nipigon, a miner, and a taxi driver, and owned his taxi company in Little Italy. He helped many immigrants whenever he could.

Nana and Papu were happy and glad they came to North America to start a new life, even though the great depression (1929 to 1939) took its toll on everyone. Then in 1939 life would change, World War II had started.

Grandpa and Grandma Early Life

Grandpa and Grandma arrived in Thunder Bay South, stayed put for a short while then decided to move the family to a little place called Mokomonn, in Comnee Township. The family moved 40 kilometers north of Thunder Bay. Grandpa worked as a camp carpenter and logger in this area until 1939. Logging was hard work. Grandpa cut timber, sized it then helped the crews drag it to the river. The wood would sit here until spring breakup. As spring came, the logs were floated to sawmills along the river. In 1924, Great Lakes Paper mill came to be which resulted in a new mouth to feed that would require a tremendous amount of timber and a healthy, stable workforce to satisfy its appetite.

By 1930, grandma and grandpa were living in a new log cabin that they had built. It was nothing special, four walls split into three rooms, but it was theirs, their home in a new country. It was a hot, dry summer. The forest surrounded their cabin. They were happy with their spot in the woods according to the information I got from Aunty Elsie. It was a secluded life, peaceful, free of storms and full of sunshine. They had some chickens, a couple of hogs and a milk cow, aunty said as far as she could remember they never wanted for anything. Then one morning grandpa could smell smoke looking out into the distance he could see the plumes of smoke and fire rising in the distance. He chatted with grandma and told her to start getting some things together in case they had to leave. Grandpa went to work. Everyone was watching and wondering. The fire was moving closer, would they be spared? On the other hand, would the fire destroy their lives leaving them to start over again? The next day grandpa came home early and told grandma it was time to move. They would run the chickens, the hogs, and the cow to Mrs. Lundquist's home. A few neighbors were looking for someplace safe to go. Mrs. Lundquist opened her home to everyone in the area that required help. It was up a hill, and the forest all around the house had cleared creating a firebreak. Grandpa and Grandma moved the livestock and the children, the smoke was thick now mom was laying in the wagon, and everyone had scarves around their mouths and noses trying to filter the smoke and make the breathing more comfortable. Grandpa told Grandma, Aunty Barb and Aunty Elsie to have a good look at their home because when the sun shines in the morning their home will no longer be there. They loaded up the carts, took what they could, and fled to Mrs. Lindquist's home. In the morning, Grandpa was right there was nothing left except a charred shell of a house. Grandpa and Grandma lived with the Lundquist s until they built their new home. They constructed their new home in the same area, complete with a firebreak. Grandma helped the Lundquist's in the garden well grandpa continued his regular logging job.

While living in this small hamlet, the family was starting to grow, Aunty Elsie born in 1926, Mae my Mom in 1928 and Aunty Lilley in 1936. My aunts and Mom attended school in Mokomonn, which was a small-secluded place, and there were not many amenities, according to my mom. I think she was the first to coin the phrase "You think you've got it tough when I was young, we walked both ways in six feet of snow all uphill on our way to school and home." I guess I couldn't get a feel for this, outdoor biffies, hauling water, and cutting firewood. Life would revolve around school and home duties.

In 1939 Grandpa's dream job became a reality. He became a carpenter for Great Lakes Paper and the family was on the move again. They moved back to Thunder Bay South and resided at 618 North Vickers Street. Grandpa and Grandma were sure that they had made the right move, even though they lived through the most desperate economic times in Canada and the great depression (1929 to 1939). Then in 1939 life would change, World War II started.

Grandpa and Grandma's house on Vickers Street.

The War Years

The war years were hard for all families. It was not long since "the war to end all wars" ended in 1918. Then 21 years later the Second World War started in 1939 when Germany invaded Poland. It was not long before Germany was in control of Europe and a multitude of countries was now in despair. Canada, being a young country still under the Commonwealth banner, was obligated to send help to Great Britain, in any manner that was required. Men went off to war, and the majority of women stayed back to help in the war effort.

My aunty Elsie worked in the munitions factory, the old Canada Starch buildings on Mission Island. The Department of Munitions purchased the old plant in 1943 and converted it to a shell packing plant for the war effort. Many Thunder Bay Old-timers knew the former facility as the "Shell Plant."

Aunty Elise wanted a job at the Canadian Car and Foundry Plant, building airplanes. She was a little ticked that my mom got a job there even though she was underage (Mom was around 16). Aunty Elsie stated that mom looked older than 16. She became one of the many "Rosie the Riveters of the north." Thousands of women from all across Canada donned trousers, packed lunch buckets, and took up the tools required to participate in the most magnificent modern war effort in Canadian history. Mom told me that she lived too far away from the plant. She left home and room and boarded at a place in Westfort, a small community adjacent to Thunder Bay South. Before the war, the Canadian Car and Foundry had an all-male workforce. During the war years, the men went off to war, and this created a shortage of workers. The availability of female personnel became essential for the workforce, and in time, they made up for 40% of the workforce. As this happened, I can proudly say that my family was involved in this effort.

Mission Island and the city of Fort William as seen in the late 1940s. At the center is the edible oils plant, originally the Fort Willam Starch Company. During the Second World War, Northern Engineering and Supply Company retrofitted the plant to produce munitions. Photo By Fryer, TBHMS 97328.41A

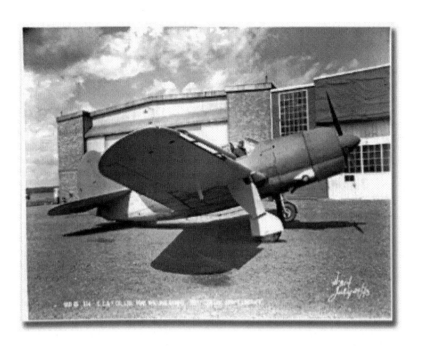

The first Curtiss SBW-1 aircraft from the Fort William
plant, Canadian Car and Foundry Co.,
July 29, 1943
Photographer unknown
Canadian Car and Foundry collection
Black and white print, Reference
Code: C 190-5-0-0-15
Archives of Ontario, I0002978

In the meantime, thousands of men joined the armed forces. During 1939 to 1945 more than 40% of the male population in Canada between the ages of 18 to 45 participated in some form of the military. Over one million people joined the war effort, virtually all of them as volunteers. Papua's boys were in the reserves except for Uncle Nick, he had flat feet, which prevented him from embarking on this journey. My dad enlisted, and if one believes in God and angels, then my dad was well-taken care of. Instead of going to Italy, dad spent his time in Jamaica at a prisoner of war camp guarding prisoners captured in the war.

Dad was one of the lucky ones. That was the story he told me, and he would not discuss the war at any length. He felt deep down it was right to save the world from Hitler's tyranny, but at the same time, the price that all the allied countries had paid was beyond what anybody thought it would be. Over 45 thousand Canadian soldiers and other personnel were never going to return home as their lives, cut short in the theater of war. This war took its toll on the population of the world. The total military deaths over this period from all combatants totaled 20.8 million personal; the civilian population suffered significant losses as well 27.3 million people. The war claimed over 48 million human beginnings. The cost to the Canadian taxpayer from 1939 to 1950 related to the war was a staggering 33 billion dollars.

During the war years, the remaining families worked and plodded along, surviving an ordeal that was unfathomable at the time. Grandpa and Grandma remained in Thunder Bay South on Vickers Street and had three more children Uncle Eric born 1940, Aunty Joyce 1941 and Uncle Wayne in 1943.

Papu and Nana continued with their family, they ranged in age from the mid-teens to mid-twenties, when the war started. In 1932 and 1933 my oldest aunts, Carmel and Rosie were married. In 1937, my youngest aunt on my dad's side was married to Domenico (Domenic) Figliomeni and moved to Schreiber, Ontario about 220 kilometers east of Thunder Bay North. By the end of the war in 1945, only my Dad and my Uncle Raymond had not married yet. The family all settled within a couple of blocks in all directions from Papu and Nana's home on Ontario Street in Little Italy. Papu kept working on the railway and Nana with some help, kept working the store on Ontario Street.

Back to Peace

May 8, 1945, was a day for humanity to rejoice. The Allies accepted the unconditional surrender of the Axis powers about a week after Adolf Hitler had committed suicide and with that, World War 2 ended. It would take many years for the world to recover from the scourge of the war. Europe was in shambles and would have to rebuild. With the end of the war, life would start getting back to a semblance of normal. The men would start returning home, some broken, some whole and some just a shell of what they once were. War was a cruel way to settle humanities differences; there was no choice as a madman was trying to rule the world. One of his principles get rid of anyone who disagreed with him.

Countries would have to rebuild after this terrible time. Canada, we were not destroyed by bombs and bullets, but the scars of war were still prevalent. Up to this period, the war effort took its toll on Canadian economics; up to the end of 1945, the war effort spent over 18.7 billion dollars with more spending to come.

Logistics in trying to get personnel from the war effort home would provide new nightmares. There were over a million individuals in Europe. They needed transportation back across the ocean and then there were the trains required to get them home again. The war was over; there was no glamor. Many Canadians were relieved, to have the war years behind them, but some veterans found that being away for so long that they couldn't go home again, couples just decided it was more comfortable to just call it quits than try to pick up where they left off. One of the many untold prices of war.

With the war over, many savored the victory, what do we do with the jobless soldiers streaming home? One of the most significant problems was how to tell the women that had taken up the most fabulous modern war effort at home, that they were no longer required to do these jobs. Places like Canada Car would go back to building buses and trains instead of planes and that the men coming back from the war effort would be getting their jobs back as promised by the government of the day. There were fears that we would enter a recession at the end of the war. The concerns evaporated as the economy boomed. Once again, a surge of immigrants helped transform a confident nation. A country with a social safety net beginning to take shape, this ended up being the start of the golden age for Canada.

Grandpa continued working at Great Lakes Paper; Aunty Barbara got married in 1944. Mom and Aunty Elise working with war effort until the war was over then they both left their jobs. With the war, ending it was time for mom and Aunty Elsie to move on. At the end of 1945, Grandpa and Grandma were 48 and 43 years old. They had young children at home and Grandpa had settled into his job at Great Lakes Paper.

Grandpa Bernhard and Grandma Estrid Later Years

Papu and Nana were 63 and 59 respectively. Their children, all grown, Uncle Raymond being the youngest was 19. At this time, Papu and Nana were slowing down a bit, and Uncle Nick took over the store on Ontario Street. The other brothers found work where they could Canadian Car, Paper Mills, and Railways.

Papu and Nana Later Years

Mom and Dad

Dad got out of the army between the fall of 1945 and end of 1946. Mom and her best friend took off and headed to Kapuskasing, Ontario more than 600 kilometers northeast of Thunder Bay. Mom would have had to be 17 or 18 at this time, and she and her girlfriend probably took the train to this little town. Once they arrived, they got jobs working at the Kapuskasing Inn. Mom I think was a bit on the wild side.

The story goes that a troop train came through and must have stopped here for meals or something. Mom saw dad, he was sitting with some friends, and she told her girlfriend that he was the one. She was going to meet him, and he was going to be her future husband. She orchestrated a meet, greet, and found out this fellow was from Thunder Bay North and on his way home. It was not too long after dad left that mom and her girlfriend packed up and headed back to Thunder Bay South. Mom had a mission she met this fellow, and he was not going to get away. Mom got a job when she got back to Thunder Bay south working at a five and dime store.

When dad got back to town, he got a job on the railway working as a car repairman. Mom and dad started to court between 1947 and 1949. Mom told me that they had a splendid time and their courtship was full of happiness. It seemed that when they were not working, they were like two peas in a pod having fun and getting into mischief, which appeared to be the order of the day. After years and months of the war, it was time to let your hair down. Dad's sidekick his younger brother Raymondo (Uncle Raymond) meet Teresa Figliomeni from Schreiber, Ontario and they were married on July 3, 1948, in Schreiber becoming the second connection to Schreiber as Aunty Edith was already living there after marrying Uncle Domenic. At this time the fun slowed down a bit, there was a proposal sometime in early 1949, and they set the date to get married, October 8, 1949. Mom was of Lutheran denomination, and the first thing that would have to happen is that she would have to convert to the Roman Catholic religion before they could get married which she did.

Tony and Mae (mom & dad) 1946 -1949

Dad enjoying life after the army

Mom waiting for Dad

*Mom and Dad enjoying an afternoon, could be
Boulevard Lake.*

Two People United

Showers and stags were the natural part of the process, although they were separate. Mom had two showers one given by Nana and Grandma along with all sisters from both sides of the family and received a kitchen suite and an electric rangette the modern method for cooking, games were played, and the participants had a delicious snack. Moms girlfriends had a second shower, it was a cup and saucer party, and she received eleven beautiful cups and saucers, games and lunch followed.

Dad's friends organized a get-together; there was all the fixing, homemade Italian Sausage, Genoa Salami, and other homemade sausage's. Different cheeses, bread, and pickled vegetables were available as well as an assortment of refreshments. Games were associated with stag's and dads favorite was Craps, he would partake in cards on occasion. At the end of the evening, Dad received a sum of money, used to purchase pots and pans.

The day finally arrived, and Mom she looked exquisite in a white satin floor-length gown with fingertip sleeves with a small train. The veil was white nylon net caught with a halo of white apple blossoms, and the jewelry that she wore to complement her dress was a small silver cross and lovely silver earrings. The flowers she so gingerly held were a dozen and a half vibrant red roses tied with a broad white satin ribbon.

Dad decked out in a new dark suit sporting a light colored shirt with a white silk tie while wearing a white carnation buttoner.

Principals In Wedding Ceremony

MR. and Mrs. Anthony Agostino were married Oct. 8 in the rectory of St. Anthony's Roman Catholic Church. The bride is the former Mae Johnson, daughter of Mr. and Mrs. B. Johnson, Fort William. The bridegroom is the son of Mr. and Mrs. J. Agostino, Ontario Street.
—Photo House—Morton.

Mom and Dad Wedding Picture from Newspaper

[33]

Uncle Raymond, dad's sidekick and was his best man, and Aunty Teresa was mom's Matron of Honor. My Cousin Clara Aunty Carmel's daughter was the flower girl she was thirteen years old. I found it strange that Aunty Teresa was mom's Matron of honor and not one of her sisters or girlfriends. Mom told me a story that it was tough integrating into an Italian family and that during this time frame even though everyone was in a new country, marriage tended to be of the same ethnic race. Aunty Teresa became mom's rock early on and helped her transform into the Italian family. Dad and Raymond were brothers as well as best friends, and Aunty Teresa became mom's non-biological sister and from what I remember her best friend.

Mom, Dad, Aunty Teresa, Uncle Raymond and Cousin Clara

The morning of the wedding, mom and her wedding party left Grandpa's and Grandma's house in Thunder Bay South and headed to St. Anthony's parish, located on the corner of Dufferin and Banning Street in Thunder Bay North. It was a lovely ceremony and took place at 11:00 A.M. Grandpa Bernhard gave the Bride to the arms of the one she loved. After the ceremony, Uncle Raymond and Aunty Teresa hosted a wedding breakfast at their small apartment that included all the grooms and brides relatives, which numbered at least thirty people. One thing I learned over time was that no matter how small a place is it seems to expand with love when welcoming family.

The old Italian Hall Fond Memories from here

A reception, held in the Italian Hall that evening at 7:00 PM to honor the new couple. The Italian community in Port Arthur built a hall in 1929. This meeting place would hold all kind's celebrations over the years. The Italian Society of Port Arthur organized and constructed the building located on Algoma Street. The Hall went through a major remodel in 1967. It was situated on the same plot of land and became known as The Italian Centennial Hall because the rebuild took place in Canadas centennial year. As time went on the society decided in 2001, it was time to build a new hall located on the same ground. The name changed to The Italian Cultural Trade Center. It houses a trading room, a member's room, and a local bar, open to all in the community. Most members are from families that originated from the southern regions of Italy, but again not confined to it. The hall has stayed faithful to its roots and stood the test of time in the same location. Over 300 people attended the reception. The best man proposed a toast to the bride. They cut the four-tiered wedding cake. The bride's girlfriends and sisters passed out the pieces. I am sure that Papu, Nana, Grandpa, and Grandma would have wondered in awe, this ceremony, lavish compared to what they had in Italy and Sweden. The remainder of the night would have include dancing and merriment; from the stories, I heard mom and dad were quite the dancers and could cut a rug with the best of them. The evening was over, and they, now united as one and ready to tackle the world

The next day mom and dad left on their honeymoon and went to Duluth, Minnesota. Stayed here for five days, arriving back in Thunder Bay North the night of October 13, 1949. They moved into their home on 350 Bay Street, a rooming house that they would run while dad worked on the railway.
The first time they entertained, Grandpa and Grandma as well as Uncle Raymond, and Aunty Teresa came over for supper. The meal consisted of steak, potatoes, and vegetables with tea and dessert following. Growing up, I remember Dad always enjoying a steak. It seemed he could eat steak every night.

New lives started, everyone was nurturing families. Life began across the ocean in two different countries.

Canada was a country full of diverse cultures and nationalities; a land of tolerance is what we came to be. Little Italy in Thunder Bay North was still the same, but other nationalities were settling in the same area which created new dynamics for a country that was finally leaving the throws of war behind.

The Block 1949 – 1950

*The block on the corner of Ontario and Bay Street,
Thunder Bay North. My first home.*

Part 2
"Tony's Joe"

My Start a New Life

The year drew to a close, mom and dad had settled into a new life dad working on the railway and mom running the rooming house (The Block). The average working wage was about $3000 per annum or approximately $1.20 per hour. The rooming house could accommodate between 20 and 30 single men at the time. There were some rooming houses in the area. The customers came from a variety of occupations, railway, lumber industry and construction industry.

A new decade started a couple of months after mom and dad were married half a century complete and the new half starting out. The world was still unsettled somewhat from the war years, as some countries were not satisfied with their bounty at the end of the war. The Soviet Union and China signed a treaty in 1950, which named Japan and the United States as enemies. The Soviet Union announced that it was in possession of an atomic bomb. The start of the cold war. On June 25, 1950, North Korea invaded South Korea, another encounter that the world did not need. Hopefully, this contact would be limited to this area and not break out into anything more significant. Therefore, at this time, we had finished two world wars: wars meant to end all wars only to enter a time when two countries on our planet had enough firepower to annihilate the world, which we knew.

Since the end of the war, prices had increased dramatically, and wages as it so often happened never kept pace. The men working for the railways wanted a 40-hour workweek vs. a 48-hour workweek and an increase of 7 to 10 cents an hour. The new rate would have increased the take-home pay of an employee marginally. The negations did not go very well; the railways in the United States were suffering from the same problems. On August 22, 1950, both Canadian Railway Corporations were on strike, goods, and services across the country ceased to move. In The United States, the same thing was about to happen, but President Truman took the step to order the Federal troops to take control of the railways thereby preventing a strike. In Canada, 124,000 men hit the bricks, and the country was slowly stopping. The government of the day passed legislation ordering the men back to work, a tactic that legislators and politicians still use today.

Life got back to normal, at the time a new house was $8,450, a liter of gas was .05 cents, a loaf of bread was .12 cents, and a kilogram of hamburger was 0.66 cents or 0.30 cents per lb.

Then a beautiful day October 6, 1950, came upon us. My life started. Mom was in the maternity ward at St Joseph's Hospital in Thunder Bay North. I do not recollect if I was daytime or night birth, but it does not matter. Just before I was born, I left the womb to check out my new surroundings. There was a lot of commotion going on as the nuns moved in and out of the room. I looked down from a suspended state at the goings-on. There was a landmark that I noticed in the harbor as I looked out the window. According to legend at one time, the port was relatively open and unprotected. Now the rock formation seems like a huge giant that laid down and protected the harbor from the vast open lake.

Sleeping Giant "Nana Bijou" protecting the harbor in Thunder Bay. A view that I will never forget.

As I sat in this suspended state looking at the lake and the rock formation, it reminded me of a famous legend, a story that needs to be told.

A peaceful Ojibway tribe lived here eons ago, they lived a bloodless lifestyle, and for this, the Great Spirit Nana Bijou, the spirit of Deep Sea Water, would reward them. Nana Bijou showed the Ojibway chief a narrow tunnel that led to a massive silver deposit. He warned the tribe that if they divulged the location of the silver deposit, he, Nana Bijou would be changed to stone.

The Ojibway became famous for their silver ornaments and this created problems with their enemies the Sioux. Some Ojibway were captured and tortured but never gave up their secret. The Sioux chiefs used treachery as they felt they had to locate the silver mine so they could have the silver for themselves. They had their most cunning scout enter the Ojibway camp. He disguised himself, as an

Ojibway, and with stealth movements, he located the mine.

One night the Sioux spy took several pieces of silver from the vein and started to head back to the Sioux camp. He stopped at a trader's post for food. He arrived at the post without furs for trading. He did have some silver for trade. The merchant's suspicion became aroused, and after some treachery, they had convinced the Sioux spy to show them where he got the silver. They left in the Sioux scout's canoe and headed to the secret location, just as they came in sight of Silver Islet, a terrific storm broke out and swamped the boat, and the traders perished. The Sioux spy was found drifting in his canoe with his mind completely lost.

A strange thing happened during the storm; once there was a full opening in the Bay, now there lays a giant sleeping figure of a man. Nana Bijou, the Great Spirit, warned that this could happen and now Nana Bijou, turned to stone.

I am told that a partly submerged shaft can be seen on occasion to what was once the most productive silver mine in the northwest. Lake Superior stands guard as many have tried to pump out the shaft to get to the silver, but it has been a lost cause to date. Is it protected by the curse of great spirit Nana Bijou the spirit of Deep Water, who can tell?

Lake Superior Facts, by surface area, the world's largest freshwater lake. Estimations show, over 30,000 men, more than 6,000 ships have met their watery grave on the great lakes. Lake Superior is known to have terrible storms in the fall that would rival hurricanes on the oceans. One of the most famous ships to be lost was the SS *Edmund*

Fitzgerald. A terrible winter storm blew up with near hurricane – force winds and waves that were topping 35 feet high on November 10, 1975, at 7:10 PM. Lake Superior claimed another victim as the 729-foot ship along with a crew of 29 and a cargo of over 26,000 tons of iron ore met their watery grave.

I returned to the womb, there was a gasp before a final push, I was born, did I pick up the spirit of mining from the Nana Bijou, who knows. Born in the fall, a Libra, the time when Lake Superior could become a monstrous body of water taking and giving as she thought fit.

The scales of justice became a stable part of my life. The number 22 according to constellations and other mysteries of life, my life path number. This figure if one believes in astrology, the value 22 is the most powerful, potentially the most successful. The Life Path number, it is often referred to as the Master Builder and provides the unique ability to see the larger picture. According to the information on hand, I could be a creator of ideas; a planner and some of my positions throughout my life could help humanity and create a better world.

Grandma Estrid was born on October 6, 1902; a great day.

"Tony's Joe" Early Years

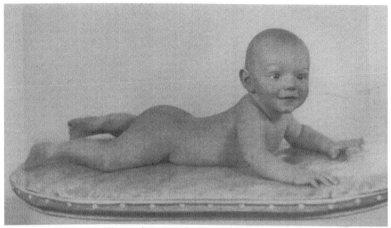

Tony's Joe" 3 months old

In 1950 Nana and Papu's children were all married, with families of their own. My extended family was growing at the time; I had 14 first cousins on the Italian side ranging in age from four to nineteen. Mom and Dad were the last to get married, and by the end of 1949, all dad's brothers and sisters were married.

On the Swedish side, the family was also growing; Aunty Barb, Aunty Elsie, and Mom had gotten married. My other aunts and uncles were still relatively young Aunty Lynn was 14, Uncle Eric 10, Aunty Joyce 9 and Uncle Wayne 7. There was a difference in family dynamics at the time. Grandpa and Grandma compared to Nana and Papu were still bringing up youngsters as well as having married daughters.

When I was born, Uncle Nicky's Joe was five; Uncle Raymond's Joe was born in Nov of 1950, and so starts the story of "Tony's Joe."

[45]

Nineteen fifty-one was an average year as I was a babe, I turned a year old, and mom and Aunty Teresa spent a lot of time with Raymond's Joe and myself. My cousin Frank, Raymond's Joe brother, was born in Nov 1951. Uncle Raymond and Dads family were starting to grow. In 1952, my brother Rick was born in May, and the other exciting thing to happen was that Nana and Papu celebrated their 50th wedding anniversary on Nov 27, with a celebration, at the Italian Hall. This was the first party that I attended in Little Italy's famous hall. The whole family was here including Arthur Squitti, Nana's adoptive son.

Not sure exactly when this happened I thought I was three years old and I had a severe illness called polio. Children's health was a constant worry for parents in the 1950s; there were epidemics of Polio and TB everywhere. Everyone feared these diseases; when I was older mom told me that I had polio and that Doctor Burnford was the one that came to my rescue and helped me recover from whatever malady that I had. I was one of the lucky ones. Everyone knew someone who suffered from one of these horrible diseases. As far as I am aware a lot of my third year was spent in and out of hospital care. I developed a taste for Kool-Aid and arrowroot cookies while in the hospital. These two favorites were the snack of the day on the children's ward. Whenever I see kids having a drink of Kool-Aid or eating an arrowroot cookie, it brings back that memory of snack time in the hospital. That was the only good memory that a child could have during those days as hospitals; were run by a regiment of rules, such as just visitors allowed during visiting hours. It was a very lonely place; a Catholic hospital with lots of nuns running the show. They were not compassionate at all. When I got out, mom said I was happy to be home, but arrowroot cookies and Kool-Aid still even to this day have a place in my heart.

In 1954 my brother Bruce was born, along with my cousin Maria, Aunty Teresa's daughter. Dad and Uncle Raymond were working on the railway and life was normal. In 1955 my cousin Leonard was born. Thinking back mom, dad, Aunty Teresa, and Uncle Raymond, we were a tight family, which included the kids. Raymond's Joe and I stayed pretty close together while Rick and Frank became childhood buds; Bruce and Leonard well it seemed like it was hard to pull them apart and Marie she was a girl, and at the time, we did not want to have anything to with her. So for the next few years, the dynamics of this group growing up in Little Italy became inseparable. With our dad's family all around us, our lives were full of fun and happiness. Trouble never actually came our way as children no matter what we got into, the family always had eyes on us. Therefore, the dynamics on dad's side, we were one huge family with a multitude of parents. Discipline would typically be handled by anyone of the parents if required.

On Moms side the family dynamics remained strained; our households were not close, not sure why but when I think back speculation is that the immigrant nationalities with different cultures and religions just did not get along.

By the end of 1955, I had on dad's side 21 first cousins ranging in age from 3 months to 23 years old. On mom's side, there were numerous first cousins all living in Thunder Bay South. When I think about it now, they might as well have been 1000 miles away instead of just the 5 miles that we were apart.

Left Side "Tony's Joe" 3 or 4 years old
Right Side "Tony's Joe" around school age notice how
happy I am.

Mom "Tony's Joe" Ricky and Dad

[48]

*"Tony's Joe" right side and Ricky sitting on block
steps*

Left to Right Rickey, Brucey, and "Tony's Joe."

[49]

Dad had a love for cars all his life.

Mom enjoyed the cars as much as dad did.

History and Technology

Nineteen Fifty to Nineteen Fifty-five were good years in Canada although there sad times, in 1952, King George VI Canada's Head of State passed away; Queen Elizabeth II was crowned the new Head of State. In 1953, the war in Korea ended. Three hundred and fourteen Canadians lost their lives while 1,211 were injured. During this period, Louis Saint Laurent was Liberal Prime Minister of Canada. He wished to transform Canada to be more involved in world affairs. He was a proponent of Canada joining NATO in 1949. St. Laurent did not like communism and as a result was far less fearful of the United States. He and Mackenzie King shared and agreed with most policies of the time. The Alberta Social Credit party was in power in Alberta. Joey Smallwood a liberal who ushered Newfoundland and Labrador into the Canadian Confederation in 1949 was leading a new province in a new direction. In Saskatchewan Tommy Douglas of the Saskatchewan, CFF party was in power. Mr. Douglas was the father of Medicare in Canada. The Saskatchewan CFF party was the forerunner to the modern day NDP. Many people in positions of power did not trust Mr. Douglas as they thought he was a communist. Many of the politicians of the day were very pro-business and anti-union at the time. Lester B Person who later became the Prime Minister of Canada. At this period he was elected to be the president of the United Nations. Some famous Canadians that were born during this time frame; Jack Layton, John Canady, Dan Aykroyd, Guy Lafleur and Lanny McDonald just to name a few.

The invention of television happened in 1927, but it took many years before it caught on. Up to 1948, in Canada, there were around 325 television sets. Thousands of television sets were purchased by working people between 1948 and 1952; estimations were high as sales, expected to reach 85,000 television sets. The sales concentration was generally in Southern Ontario. The average TV at the time ranged in price from 200 to 290 dollars, these, black and white models with small screen were like pieces of furniture. CBC entered the Canadian television market in 1952. Some of the programs that aired at the time are Holiday Ranch, aired in 1953 was an everyday variety program with country music. How About That with Percy Saltzman broadcast in 1953 was a 15-minute science show for children. Then in 1954 Howdy Doody aired. The CBC rewrote the program. It went from an American version to the Canadian version.

Hockey Night in Canada got its origin in 1952 with one game on Saturday nights. Rene Lecavalier called the first game in Montreal for the CBC's French-language television network. This game played at the Montreal Forum, between old rivals, Montreal Canadians and the Detroit Redwings. Three weeks later on November 1, 1952, Foster Hewitt called the first game for the CBC English network between the visiting Boston Bruins and the Toronto Maple Leafs from the Maple Leaf Gardens. For the 1952/1953 season, Con Smyth sold the rights for one year at $100 per game, as he wanted to see how well received, this TV game thing would be. It proved to be a phenomenal success. After the season, he sold the rights for the next three years for a total of $150,000. In the early 1960's he sold the television rights for the next six years for 9 million dollars; he netted an average of $21,000 per game.

Therefore, at the end of 1955, the average wage at the time was just over $4,000 per year, average 2 dollars per hour. Housing was around $10,000, a liter of gas was .055 cents, a loaf of bread was .17 cents, and a kilogram of hamburger was 0.79 cents or 0.36 cents per lb. Now, as far as I can remember we didn't have a TV set.

Then 1956 rolled in. For the majority of the year, I was just a kid. Playing around in Little Italy. Later in the fall of the year, I started school.

School My First Two Days

The first five years were enjoyable being just a kid. Now as fall approaches in 56, I am heading towards my sixth birthday, what adventures would be in store for me.

As a youngster in Little Italy, I felt utterly safe; being a child vanished with each passing day.

Now in the fall of the year, it was time to start school. I was about to enter Saint Joseph's School; it was time to start a new journey and a new adventure, not sure what was in store. Once you enter school, childhood innocence ceases to exist, a new life ahead, where will it lead.

The very first day of school mom walks with me. We came around the corner; I looked up at the massive building in front of me. Gates and fences were there to meet me as we passed through into the schoolyard. There in front of mom and myself are the gaping doors that lead into the depths of the building. The walls must have been at least six feet thick, and the windows were high and unbreakable, at least that is how it looked to a small boy. As we passed through the doors into the unknown, I was trembling with fear or excitement not sure which. In a few seconds, I let go of mom's hand. Standing there with tears in my eyes, I realized, it was now time to become a big boy.

Looking down the hallway, one of my worst fears came to be a Nun (Penguin) was coming towards us. In this vast hall of learning the Penguins were the teachers, I remembered them well from my hospital days; this was the second time I encountered them in all their blaze and glory.

I was about to be passed off to a stranger, a penguin who would be my disciplinarian for the next 9 to 10 months. I stood there; building up all the courage a small boy could muster and turned around, and mom was gone. Thinking to myself it is time to step up and be a man. How often have I heard that term, used those words throughout my life? It is wrong to rob children of their innocence, so early I was heading to my 6 birthday, now was entering a journey of learning that will last a lifetime. Today we send innocent young children to the halls of learning at an even younger age.

Before long, the commotion of that first day was over. I did not like it one bit and was not a happy soul. I looked out through the large doors; mom was standing there ready to walk me home. Tomorrow will be a different day as I would be on my own.

Day 2 came; I made my way to the school wandering the streets I knew so very well, this was part of my neighborhood, it is friendly here, the family in Little Italy watch over you. I then turned the corner, no one is holding my hand, and the building is standing there like a gigantic gargoyle waiting to swallow me up. Pass through the gate, and head towards the massive double doors. Once I enter these hallowed halls, the wonders of the world will fill my brain.

Once again, I was not a happy camper these nuns who were supposed to be full of compassion and love, I found were miserable and unpredictable in their actions. The day would start by lining up outside, then entering the school; the Penguins expected us to be quiet. Once we passed through the massive dark doors, be quiet we were told, as talking was not allowed. The only noise the Penguins wanted to hear was the shuffling of tiny feet on the cold hard granite floor on the way to the classroom. Being taught at a very young age that they were there to educate and I was there to learn. They would carry out this task, as it did not matter to them if you were in grade one or eight they were the boss. The Nuns were capable of handing out discipline as needed, and they did not blink an eye. The older boys filled us younger kids in on what would happen if we misbehaved.

My school adventure started, and for the next two years, it was no fun. I think I was afraid of the nuns or possibly just shy. With this attitude, the sisters figured that I was not very bright and they just pushed me to the back of the classroom. At the end of grade two, I passed into grade three, but the nuns warned mom and dad that I was not the learning type, and I was slow, but they passed me anyway as I was moving to a new school and would no longer be their problem.

A typical school in the 50's, institutions large cold forbidding buildings. Halls of knowledge, motto "you will learn." The ramifications, many a tear were shed.

Part 3
Little Italy to the Farm

The Move

During this time mine and Raymonds Joe's life revolved around school. Sometime during the summer of 58, we moved out of Little Italy. A plot of ground on John Street Road became or new home. My family from little Italy seemed to be a distant memory. I finished grade one and two, left Little Italy and Raymonds Joe, to a world of unknowns for a small boy.

I do not know what necessitated the move and never will as that secret went with the passing of mom and dad, through the years the story was never told.

The land was marginal at best when I think about it today. We had between 2.5 and 3 acres of land that we were going to try and eke out a living. The house by today's standards would have been a tar paper shack. It was between 600 to 800 square feet no running water, wood stove in the kitchen. It had a total of four rooms, bedroom for mom and dad, a living room complete with an old oil space heater and no television. The kitchen came complete with a wood-burning cookstove, just off the kitchen was a pantry that housed goods, an icebox and bunk beds for myself and my two brothers. Remembering on Saturday night was bath night, the old wash tub, the water heated up on the stove and then a quick bath clean for church on Sunday morning. I was young, and we became a tight family. Looking back on that house and that land we were just sharecroppers. We had a simple, loving life maybe we just didn't know any better. The world was made up of two classes, those who had everything they could want and more. The rest of us eked out a living, but we had families, that we loved and they loved us, I do not ever remember going to bed hungry. When we left Little

Italy, myself, and my brothers were very young, I was at the most seven and half years old, and my brothers were younger than that. What a commotion it must have been to uproot the family and move to the country. Here we got set up on this small piece of ground to start a life. Dad, I think loved it I know Papu did he would want to visit every day. So we had a large potato patch set up a small hog breeding operation and a rabbit hutch. We sold vegetables, piglets that were 3 months old to a more significant hog operator and the rabbits were being sold to our Italian friends as this was somewhat of a delicacy. Not sure why we moved, but we did, and I feel this was the first of many curveballs that were thrown at me during my life.

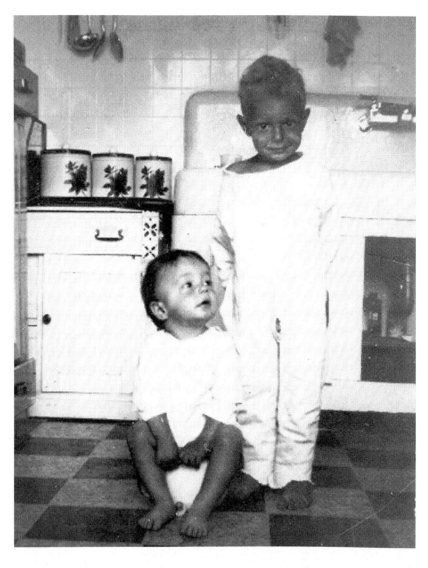

Ricky and Joey in old house amenities just were not there, but it was full of love

Joe and the Rabbits

The rabbit hutch was one of the first things we started on our farm. Raising rabbits was not a lucrative business, but it was a delicacy among Italians, so we were rearing rabbits and selling them to our friends. Our hutch had a multitude of colored rabbits white, black and two-toned. One day I was walking by the rabbit hutch, and my little mind, which was still getting used to this country living lifestyle was telling me there was something wrong with these colored rabbits.

My knowledge of a farm and farm animals was negligible and thinking today it was nonexistent. I stopped and was looking at these rabbits in their pens. When dad was selling them, the white were the ones everybody wanted they were the best. What I didn't realize was that the white rabbits seemed to be larger than the rest. How did these other rabbits get so dirty? As I was looking at them, I thought about the other rabbits that we learned about in school they were white in the winter and two-toned or dirty in the summer from possibly playing in the dirt.

I thought I am going to help dad and wash these rabbits so that he could sell them to. I noticed a full pail of water sitting very near the hutch and a plan came to be, dad would be so proud of me. I caught a two-toned rabbit and took him out of the pen, grabbed him by the ears and started to dunk him in the pail, he was squealing and making funny sounds, and he got away from me and ran. So I figured we will try this one more time. I caught the second rabbit and proceeded over to the pail, was ready to start dunking. Dunked once and the rabbit got agitated and somehow bit me. I was flabbergasted that the rabbit nipped me and I was in tears as I ran to the house.

Mom and Dad wanted to know what had happened. I explained to them how this unfortunate incident came to be. I just wanted the rabbits to be white so they would be easier to sell. By the look on dad's, face I knew I was in trouble. Dad explained to me that the rabbits come in many different colors and it's okay for them to be different. Punishment still had to be handed out for letting them out of their pens. Dad and I went up to the hutch, caught the rabbits that I let loose and put them back in their cage. Dad showed me how to clean the pens, make sure the rabbits had food and water, this was my job for the next week. I learned a few valuable lessons. Just because the rabbits have brown fur that doesn't mean they are dirty. Learned how to clean and take care of the rabbits and rabbits do not need a bath.

Dad's Accident

This incident happened late summer or early fall of 58. This affected our lives, dad had a terrible accident when he was working on the railway. As a little boy, my life revolved around school, home, Little Italy and the farm. One night we were gathered up, and we had to go and stay at Uncle Jimmy's on Algoma Street. He had an apartment that we could look out the window onto the street below. Remembering that night as myself and Rick looked out the window and were just amused and amazed by the amount of traffic on the road. It was something to watch, it seemed like there was a continuous line of cars and trucks. This was a busy area in town compared to Little Italy, and there was far more traffic here than on John Street.

Rick and I were oblivious to what was going on, but every time we came into the kitchen, there was a hush that occurred over the room. Then the next day we understood what had happened Dad had an accident and was in the hospital. He was working trying to repair a boxcar door I think Uncle Raymond was working with him. They tried to maneuver the door back in place, it slipped, all hell broke loose, as it fell to the ground. Uncle Raymond managed to scamper out of the way, but the door slammed down on dad's back, pinning him to the ground. Later we learned that dad had a broken back, no one knew if he was going to walk again, we thought he might have to be in a wheelchair. The family was there, and everyone was scared. I must have been scared to, just because everyone else was afraid. To someone as young as I was this was a time in my life when I was not sure what to think, or how it would affect us.

The angels were with dad again on this occasion, he had his operation to fix his back. The doctors, I learned at a later time had fused two of his vertebrae together, and the prognosis was good. When we finally got to see dad, he was in a body cast. I remember that someone sat me on his stomach, but it didn't hurt him as dad was in a full body cast from his shoulders to his toes. He said he was well taken care of, but I didn't believe him because all those nuns were running around again. Remembering them from my hospital stay and from school. The doctors came in, and they poked his toes with a needle to see if he had any feeling. Mom told us later that he could feel this. That meant, I learned then, dad was not paralyzed, and he would be able to walk again. Everyone was relieved. When I saw dad for the second time, he told me to help mom on the farm, with a nod, he understood I would. He was down in the dumps a little bit, and I told him to try the kool-aid and the cookies that would make him feel better.

Dad got transferred to Toronto where he did rehab on his back and learned to walk again. It was a lonely time for us out on our little plot of land. With dad laid up with his back mom, myself and my brothers were trying to eke out a living on this ground. There were many days that we all wondered how things were going to turn out. This was a time when the families all pulled together, we had an enormous amount of help from both sides, it seemed that the Swede's and the Italians could get along after all as they all came to help us out. Papu loved the farm, maybe this was part of his dream being fulfilled when he left Italy he wanted a little piece of land, but he couldn't afford it. He was around 75 at this time and would get a ride out to our place, and he would spend the whole day on this little farm he let it be known he was the boss. I got a ride to and from school, and when I got home, there were chores to do. Uncle Nick allowed us to charge groceries at his store for the necessary supplies that we needed. We were somewhat self-sufficient, I guess that was a bonus living on the farm. Dads brothers all helped when they could. It was different time as mom didn't even have a driver's license. Mom's younger brother Uncle Eric who was 16 or 17 at the time also came out every day to help with chores before and after school. With all the help we stayed afloat, sold piglets vegetables and rabbits, life was not grand, but it was tolerable. Mom needed to get her driver's license so we could be more independent. One of the neighbors decided that he would be able to teach her how to drive that was a story unto itself.

Mom's Driving Lesson

Mom needed her license to be able to go to town and get groceries and other supplies that we required. It was a lonely life, living the life of poor sharecroppers on this piece of ground without dad around. Well now this woman who built planes during the war years, moved 600 kilometers east in Ontario to find work after the war, then took it upon herself to get her husband all before she was 19 years old. She needed a driver's license this would be a lifeline, so decided now was the time to get one.

Now after all that has happened, she decided it was time to master the mechanics of the old Fargo truck, Old Blue, learn how to drive and in the process get her drivers licenses. How hard can it be? This would create independence and some freedom. The old truck was a beautiful looking truck, blue in color.

The day arrived for the first driving lesson, I was watching from around the house out-of-the-way not sure how this was going to turn out. Mom and her teacher climbed into the truck and went through the formalities including the checklist that had to be completed. Before she could bring old blue to life by turning the key and stepping on the starter, these procedures had to be completed I am sure mom thought nothing of this as she built airplanes, what could be so hard the checklist is now complete and mom getting ready to initiate contact. Mom turned the key and pressed on the starter, and the truck roared to life. The neighbor who is teaching mom had the look of relief on his face.

The second step was to get Old Blue into gear and moving. Mom stepped on the clutch and slowly put the truck into first gear. Under her instructor's tutelage, she gave the Old Blue some fuel, and the engine roared quietly as she slowly let the clutch up the gears engaged and the vehicle moved forward. After doing, this for a few times, it was time to try the exact scenario and drive in reverse. I was watching, and this was boring. Lesson number one was complete, and it was time for lunch, the neighbor said he would be back in the afternoon for lesson number two. I could hardly wait I thought we might go for a ride today.

A couple hours later the neighbor showed up for lesson number two, mom and the instructor climbed in, and I asked if I could sit in the truck box and go for a ride too. Both mom and her instructor, said no but for different reasons, mom was still nervous, and the neighbor stated that they were just going to work on the same things that they worked on the morning. I was disappointed but thought I would watch for a while, in case they changed their minds. This should be a carbon copy of the morning instructions, I thought to myself this should be a piece of cake as mom did so well in the morning. So I was sure we would be going for a ride very soon.

Mom and the instructor climbed into the cab of the truck, and I could see by looking in the window that they were going over the checklist one more time. With this process complete, mom turned the key on, and then stepped on the starter, the truck purred to life. The instructor was looking out the window at me not really paying any attention as this was lesson was going well, he told mom to put in the clutch put the truck in gear give it some gas and release the clutch and slowly move forward. Old Blue was just about to

[67]

move, and the inevitable happened, mom put the machine in gear, ahead she thought, but it was in reverse, I was watching what could go wrong, it was the same lesson as in the morning what could go wrong. Just as the truck was going to start moving the instructor felt the truck go in the wrong direction ever so slightly and yelled at mom to stop. The scream startled mom, and she panicked.

Then all hell broke loose, moms foot slipped off the clutch, the truck jumped in reverse, she stepped on the gas instead of the brake and Old Blue roared to life. The vehicle was moving in the wrong direction as fast as it could and shot across John Street into the ditch on the other side and became bogged in the mud and ground to a halt. The look of fear, on the neighbors and moms face, was priceless. They got out of the truck both trying to figure out just what had happened. After a lot of discussions and no real resolve, the neighbor decided he was not and could not help mom with her driving lessons. Another friend saw it happening came over with his tractor, and a chain, the instructor and the neighbor hooked up the truck and pulled it out of the ditch and back into our yard. Old Blue, declared the winner of this battle, mom, was in tears as she figured out this might be the end of her driving lessons and the end of her driving career. A few days later after everything calmed down a friend of dads who was an extremely patient man had heard of our predicament from my uncles and decided he could teach mom how to drive he was excellent, soon mom was driving, she got her drivers license. It's funny how different episodes change the dynamics of one's life. The day mom got her license her blue eyes sparkled like diamonds she was my hero. Thank goodness that they wouldn't let me ride the box that day. It could've had a dramatic

[68]

turn of events instead of just old blue getting stuck in the mud.

Dads Old Farm Truck.

Better Times

Dad was able to walk, he came home sometime in 1957. Dad took up his duties back on the farm, but he was not able to resume his duties on the railway. He was laid off, why, not sure, speculating his back wouldn't hold up to the rigorous work schedule. Faced with adversity, he knew he had to become a full-time farmer and work this little plot of land so he could provide for his family.

I remember at one time we had 60 hogs, some beef cattle, up to 2000 roosters all on this 3-acre plot of land, by today's standard this is an acreage, not a farm and we eked out a living. It was hard work, but we survived.

By the end of 1957 grandpa had retired from Great Lakes Paper at 60 years old, his lungs were not in good shape from his years of breathing sulfate fumes on the job. Grandma was 55 and had to take up a position doing janitorial work while still living on Vickers Street North.

Dad's mom and dad, Nana, and Papa who are 75 and 71 respectively were still living on Ontario St. and uncle Nick was running his store on Ontario Street as well as the one on Algonquin Avenue. Papu as long as he could get a ride still continue to come out to the farm a place that he loved.

In spring of 58, we settled into our new life farming 3 acres, eking out a living. Dad was home, and life was semi-normal. I was finishing Grade 2 at St. Josephs, and in the fall of the year, I would be attending a new school in our new neighborhood. Dad was mobile now, and we still had his brothers. They came out and helped as required.

I remember how this changed my life. Gone were the days of wandering up and down the streets of little Italy with Raymond's Joe. When dad got hurt, I had to grow up fast and help on the farm where I could. It was a learning curve, it never bothered me in my future endeavors. As a result, it gave me strength and a new work ethic.

In the spring of the year, the school was complete and was named Holy Cross; it was only 1.7 kilometers from home. The school itself was a modern day structure; it did not have the stern monolith look of the structures that I was used to. The school itself was tiny, consisted of three classrooms, principal's office and washrooms, no penguins (nuns) from what I heard and I thought that was a good thing. During the first year, about 60 students would be in attendance ranging from grades 1 to 8, principal, three teachers, and the custodian/bus driver. Things were starting to look up, but I was not sure about moving to another new school with new kids, and my friend Raymond's Joe would not be there.

During the summers, until we got a little older, we were allowed to go and spend a couple of weeks at Aunty Rosie's camp on Ishkibbible Beach. This particular beach was located around the point from the old Abitibi Paper Mill on Lake Superior. The cottage itself was a very rustic building but had windows on the front with the view of the sleeping giant. It was the perfect place to spend a couple of weeks the lake was always cold, but we swam anyway, and the beach was okay although at times it was filled with sawdust and wood bark depending on how the wind blew. It was only 15 kilometers from home, but it felt like we traveled to an entirely different part of the country. Once you were there, you could look out at the vast expanse of water and see ships coming in from all over the world loading grain from one of the many elevators that dotted the lake shore.

Dad had a car now too, it made our trips to town, and other places much more comfortable than sitting in the box of old blue. The significant trips that I remember as a youngster, going to Schreiber to visit dad's sister Aunty Edith and Uncle Domenic and the clan of cousins who resided in Schreiber. This was approximately 200 kilometers east and would take a couple of hours which seemed like an eternity. Dad would get someone to look after the farm, as we would go on this adventure. We traveled along the old highway, there were lots of places to be explored along the way, Nipigon, Red Rock, and Rossport just to name a few. The trip along the shore of Lake Superior had exquisite scenery, to this day, rivals much of what I have seen throughout my life. Then once we got there would be food and fun galore waiting for us. Pasta, sausage all homemade, smiles, and love that would keep us until the next visit. Sleeping, well just stand the mattress up, lay on the floor like cordwood go to bed get up and have fun all over again, some of the best trips were when Uncle Raymond and Aunt Teresa visited at the same time. Then the trip home never seemed so long, as it was full of stories and smiles all the way home. Get home get the chores done and wait for the next adventure, two hours from home, well that was like going to the other side of the world.

When dad got home from the hospital, we did some exploring in the area, and the summer of 58, we discovered McIntyre Creek. There were three areas to

[72]

swim in the creek all within 1/2 mile from home. Baby falls a small set of rapids going into a shallow pool, we discovered this, but it was not for us. Just downstream, there was a place called girl falls again the rapids were gentle here, the rocks were worn smooth you walk up the current sit down in the rapids, and it was like a water slide back into the pool. This was a larger pool of water that averaged about 4 feet deep. When we went to go to the creek on our own, we went to this spot.

I remember catching crayfish here boiling them in an old tobacco can, a little salt, and pepper and we thought we were eating like kings. The same spot where I had my first cigarette, dried leaves rolled up in newsprint. Lite it up, took a huge drag, thought I was going to die never tasted anything so harsh. Mom's cigarettes were far better.

The last spot on the creek, boys falls, a larger and steeper set of rapids dumping into a pool of considerable size and has a depth of 5 to 10 feet. There was a spot on the rocks, a natural place to jump off the cliffs into the pool below. The jump was between 7 and 10 feet and used by everyone.

During the summer of 58, this became the bathtub with dad, on Saturday evenings if the weather happened to be warm down to the creek we would go; get cleaned up, then head back home. Bathed and ready for church on Sunday morning. We spent many a summer day there.

The summer of 58 was a good one. Dad was home from the hospital, and the farming life we were enjoying was starting to pay dividends, even though they were small. Our tarpaper shack was our castle, it did not have many amenities, but it was full of love.

At this time, dad and mom decided that if we were going to continue this adventure, a new home would be required. They agreed on plans for a new house, this would be built in 58 and 59 with all of the modern day amenities, a proper furnace, indoor plumbing and running water and even a television in the living room. We boys would have our own bedroom.

Our new house on the farm. "Tony's Joe's" room on the second floor above the big window. Had all the amenities. Tar paper shack to our new digs.

New School

Since we moved out to the country one area that fell short, there was no Catholic school and no penguins (Nuns) to be found I thought that was a plus. In 1956, a group of parents decided to speak to father St. James about a Catholic school in the area, they gathered names of people who would support a Catholic school, talked to the Ministry of Education and received permission and funding necessary to build the school.

Holy Cross School a nice modern looking school, compared to the large monolith type buildings.

Rick and I both started school at Holy Cross in the fall of 58, I was in grade 3, Rick was in grade 1. We took the bus, and it picked us up right outside our door, we thought that was pretty neat. I believe this was the last winter that we spent in our little home. Going to the new school was okay, not lots of money for anything, so we had a lot of clothes that were passed down. It was all right we still looked pretty sharp. There were day's though some of the kids would make fun of us. Sometimes we would wear the same thing for a couple of weeks, but they were always clean. It was a different school, sort of two classes, them and us, we were not the only poor kids in school. I remember some of the kids that thought they were from the right side of the tracks and therefore better than us, telling us that we were just miserable brats. One kid, in particular, said our parents were D.P.'s and Dagoes. I had no idea what this meant and just shrugged it off. I knew it was not a good thing and that I would talk to dad about it when the time presented itself. I had a hard time fitting in again, Rick was doing great, and he really liked school.

My third-grade teacher was a dedicated teacher, an early lesson that she taught me was that I would only get out of school what I put into it, if I didn't want to work then I would just stay in the same grade until I decided I had had enough. She was different though instead of putting me at the back of the class like the Penguins had done for two years, I had to sit at the front of the room where she could keep an eye on me. Goofing off was not an option, I had to pay attention, or there would be trouble. I did not actually learn what I was supposed to learn my first two years, so I was struggling at this new school from day one. Although I was not a star student at the time, I knew I would have to develop a good work ethic, while working hard to succeed.

I was having a hard time fitting in, a new school to contend with, and new teachers and then realizing that we were poor by the standards of the day. Life was so simple in Little Italy we did not have much of anything either, but we had a family, and the place was full of love.

There was this one kid in school, and for some reason, he took it upon himself to make my life miserable even more miserable than I thought it possibly could be. He continued with the name-calling, I was a D.P. immigrant and dago. Finally, I went home and asked my dad to explain what a D.P. and a dago was. The look that came across his face frightened me, where did you hear that. I explained to him what was happening at school. He sat me down and explained what a dago was; first, he told me it was a sign of disrespect for our nationality. The other term was D.P.; Dad said that these were primarily displaced people from World War II camps. They came across the ocean to find a new life much like Nana and Papa in the early 1900s, Dad explained we were Canadian, born in Canada and were of Italian descent, we were not displaced people, but Canadians. A particular core of Canadians was upset that they were allowing more immigrants into the country. Dad said we were a country of immigrants and there should be no name calling as these people are just trying to find a place where they could be free.

About a week later at school this fellow came and started with the name-calling again, funny thing though, he was of Italian descent. The name-calling seemed to make him feel good or give him some sort of power over other people. We were enjoying recess one day when the name-calling started again, and I asked him to stop, he continued on, so I told him to stop, or he would be sorry. He laughed at me and called me a D.P. dago, I looked at him and mustered up all the strength I could find, then shot towards him with all my weight and tackled him to the ground. We wrestled a bit, and he got away, he stood up, I jumped up as he came at me with fists swinging, one caught me, smacked me on the jaw, staggered me a bit. As he came at me again, I struck him with a jab, a move

[77]

that I learned at boxing lessons. The punch hit him square in the nose, and his nose started to bleed. This startled him, and he ran to the teachers I felt good about myself. Once the bleeding stopped, up to the principal's office, and after hearing what had happened, the principal informed us that fighting would not be tolerated. The punishment dealt out; both given the strap. The second part of the penalty was we had to tell our parents what had happened at school. I knew this was going to be worse than the strap. I explained to mom and dad what had happened at school when I got home. I did get a spanking, the second punishment; this was the norm for the day. It seemed that if you got into trouble at school, you were in trouble at home. Dad explained to me that fighting was not going to be tolerated. In my little boy's voice, I related my position that this kid was calling me names. Dad's answer to this was, "did the names break any bones." He made his point even though I did not agree with him at the time, he was the boss, and my dad and I still loved him.

Well, the end of the year came about, and the teacher informed mom and dad that I would have to redo grade three. There were some reasons, but I just did not have the knowledge to succeed in fourth grade, at this time if you did not learn you stayed put until you had the required knowledge to succeed in the new grade. I finished school that year, and there was no more name-calling. When school was completed, the kid that I got into a fight with, had moved away, and I never heard from him again.

Christmas Eve With Grandpa and Grandma

We found ourselves to be very close to our family on Dads side. We were never really close to the family on mom's side. After all the help that we received from mom's side during that trying time when dad was in the hospital, Dad said we would have to get closer to the folks on mom's side. How would we do this, we would spend Christmas Eve with the relatives on mom's side. This became known as the sock party between myself and dad, I overheard dad say to mom one Christmas Eve, "come on Mae lets get going we do not want to be late for the sock party" I let it pass, but before we got into the house I asked dad what he meant. He told me "I was not supposed to hear that comment," but he said "you have to keep this to yourself" and I said "okay." Dad said, "I always get a pair of socks for a Christmas present from your mom's side of the family, ever since I meet your mom that was a standing gift." I said "swell," and then dad said, "when we go into the house there will be a smell, it smells like old dirty socks, it's not, it's just Grandma Estrid cooking her Lutefisk." Well, we walked in the door, I knew grandma was cooking something that had a harsh smell, but this night it was unusually high, the smell of fish was overpowering. I learned later that having lutefisk was a tradition as well as a delicacy. This fish is dried cod that is soaked in a lye solution to rehydrate the fish for some days. Once this step is complete, the fish is then doused and rinsed for several more days to get rid of the lye solution, this was done for another five or six days with the water being changed daily. Once this part of the process was complete, the fish was either baked or boiled them served with butter and salt and pepper. I never had to eat any, and the smell told me it would have tasted like the cod liver oil I was given every morning, and that was bad enough.

So Christmas Eve at grandma and grandpas did bring our family a little closer together. The evening consisted of a gift exchange the little kids always had to go upstairs so Santa could come and put the gifts under the tree. When we were allowed to come down, we would all get a gift, a small one as no one had a lot of money, so the socks I learned later were an excellent present considering the era. To this day, I do not know how Santa made it to this house on Christmas Eve. When I talked to Raymonds Joe on Christmas Day, he told me Santa didn't come to his house until after they were sleeping, a mystery. Once the gifts were opened, then dinner would be served. The traditional meal consisted of lutefisk, of course, mashed potatoes, Swedish meatballs, ham, and turkey. One other item that was always on the menu was Kropkakor, "Pault," Swedish potato dumplings a real highlight for Scandinavian's who have grown up with this dish. It was a simple dish served with butter and salt and pepper. It was a cheap meal, and we had it many times at home not just on the holidays, it was a staple in grandma and grandpa's house as well as our own place. To this day I still have a hankering for Swedish meatballs and pault. That gross fish odor well that could kill any appetite I had. I thought I would never eat fish.

Grandpa at the time was on oxygen, and he was not as spry as he used to be, laid back on the couch and enjoyed everyone's company. That was the first time that someone in my family was not doing well. I didn't realize it then, I was watching, someone slowly die. This custom of having dinner at grandma and grandpas didn't last, within a few years moms side of the family was starting to scatter to different parts of the country. Dad's family stayed in and around Thunder Bay.

Grandpa Bernhardt and Grandma Estrid celebrating a birthday. "Tony's Joe" looking on.

Grandma and Grandma around 1960 - 1965.

Christmas at grandma's Brucey, Rickey behind and cousin Myles. 1960 to 1963

The following is an expert from a letter Ricky received from mom on March 17, 1991. Ricky asked mom for her pault recipe, and this is what she replied.

Here's the recipe for pault.

Potatoes, try to get older ones, cause there not as starchy.
Boil, mash add one or two eggs depending on the number of potatoes you have.
Add flour, enough to hold potatoes together, also this depends on the number of potatoes you have.
Before you cook the potatoes fry salt pork and onions in a pan together.
Have them and your pot of salted water boiling before you mix the dough.
Once you mixed the dough, make the pault as fast as you can, because the dough starts to get soft and your pault will turn out too mushy.
As you put pault in the boiling water, keep the lid on the pot, so they won't stop boiling.
When they float to the top cook for another ten minutes or so.
Do not overcook cause they'll fall apart.
You can use flour on your hands to roll them, but I find if you use cold water on your hands to roll them it works better.
By the way, just let the potatoes after mashed cool just enough so you can mix the dough with your hands.
So this is all I can tell you about making pault.
Good luck, let me know how they turn out, have a good day and give the kids a hug for me.

Love Mom

Now what she forgot, is the pault are stuffed with the salt pork mixture then sealed and rolled. The size of a pault was about two and a half to three inches in diameter. When cooked serve with a copious amount of butter and pepper.

Other stuffing we have used over the years are Italian sausage, family recipe and or bacon and onions.

Ingredients
16 cups of mashed, shredded or use a potato ricer to rice potatoes.
2 eggs.
4 cups of flour used as needed.
1 lb salt pork.
2 large onions.

From the pot to the plate sliced or chopped covered with copious amounts of butter. I thought they were delicious.

The Farm A New Direction

Nineteen fifty-nine was a transition year on the farm. During the winter of 58/59, the pork operation was the only thing that we had on the go. We were raising the piglets for a more significant pork operator.

In the spring of 59, dad decided we had to have a few more options to make a living on our little piece of land. He decided we would move in a different direction, gone were the rabbits and vegetable garden, it was replaced with roosters and cattle. The hog production kept us busy year round as we would try to get two litters of piglets per year. That would total up to around 160 piglets, about 80 piglets in the early part of the year and then another batch in late fall. Dad then decided to get some beef cattle 6 or 7 Hereford calves, picked up in the early spring at the auction and sell them either in the late fall or through the winter months. The last to go where the rabbits they were okay, but they were a lot of work for the income we received.

When dad's compadres asked dad if he had any chickens for sale, we always had a few, but when our hen's were not laying eggs, they ended up in our freezer then into homemade spaghetti sauce.

Dad looked at the idea of raising roosters, get them in the spring, let them grow through the summer and then sell in the early fall. Our barn was a big two-story concrete building about thirty feet wide and maybe sixty feet long. We modified the loft in the barn, and with some minor repairs, this became the chick nursery. Dad would purchase a large number of rooster chicks in the early spring, we would house them in the loft until they were five to eight weeks old. We transferred them outside, where we fed and watered them until ready for market. Fresh, young roosters seemed to be the newest commodity that the Italian's wanted; our clientele was at least 90% Italian.

We had a milk cow, old Betsy, she provided us with milk and cream, we made our own butter, everyone took their turn on the butter churn to make butter.

Before dad got hurt, the farm consisted of hogs, rabbits, and vegetables. Now in 59 we had, pigs, beef cattle usually about 6 or 7, and many roosters in the summer, a milk cow, and some chickens. We were self-sufficient, meat, milk, and eggs as well as vegetables from the garden. With the roosters on site, we needed an area for them. The potato patch disappeared, we did not grow vegetables to sell anymore, but we still had a large vegetable garden for ourselves.

Papu was a regular fixture on the farm, he made sure that we had a vegetable garden; complete with all the necessary vegetables that a person could want or not want including endive, something he loved. Papu had his own backyard garden on Ontario Street it was immaculate like a picture out of a horticulture magazine. When in town we would help him pull weeds and then when he visited us on the farm he was the taskmaster at making sure that we had our garden in shape.

Boxcar Cleaning

To transport the grain from the west to the east the railway used boxcars. The grain, deposited in the elevators that dotted the shores of Lake Superior around Thunder Bay. With all the stock running on this little piece of land, we needed a variety of feed. Somehow, dad got permission to clean boxcars. Sometimes during the summer months, dad would take me to give him a hand. This is where I learned how to clean boxcars. Dad would have the location for a string of cars on the waterfront that he was allowed to sweep. Where dad received this information from I am not sure. To this day, I am confident that this arrangement was just a local agreement between my father and the local management. He must have got the location of the cars for cleaning from someone maybe the yardmaster.

The boxcars on the inside were all wood lined, and there was about a 4-inch gap between the wood lining and the steel outside shell. The walls were not sealed, and the space between the wall and the steel shell would fill with grain as the car was loaded for transport. We would loosen off the board just above the floor, and this would allow the trapped feed that we required to flow onto the floor. We would clean 10 to 20 cars per day, and it would give us 12 and 16 bushels of grain. To get the grain, each boxcar had to be swept. The feed was then gathered and dumped into the box of old blue. Once complete we would head home, and offload our treasure. Dad did this almost every day going on for some years. Thinking back this was a great way to gather feed for the stock, without this, we would have never been able to acquire the feed we required for the farm. This hard work helped with our survival. On our way back to the farm we would pick up Papu, he would come out for the day this was part of the ritual, and he loved every moment. Otherwise, Papu would sit out on the side of his house on a bench, watch, and talk to the people going by. This, dad felt was the least he could do for his father, by 1960 Papu was entering his 78th year. I think the daily farm trips kept him young.

Papu and Dad sitting outside his house on Ontario Street discussing world problems

Papu's Doctor Visit

There was a story dad told me about papu. Not feeling well in his mid-60's he begrudgingly went to see a doctor. They ran a pile of tests. They called him back in for his results; dad and one of his other sons went with him for an appointment. The news was not good. Dad said that the doctor told papu that he would have to change his lifestyle if he wanted to live longer. Papu was by no means a drinker, a glass of homemade wine at lunch and one at night when he was outside enjoying the one cigar he allowed himself each day.

The orders from the doctor were devastating, no more cigars, no wine, no homemade cold cuts or pasta.

The bland diet that the doctor suggested was not a hit. Dad said Papu's face went white when he figured out what the doctor requested of him. He asked the doctor what his life expectancy would be without quitting everything he loved. The doctor told him probably two to three years max. Papu thought for a moment, and then quietly said I will not stop, I am going to enjoy my life to the fullest with the people and the things I love most. Papu went on to live many more years he was entering his eighty-fifth year when he passed away, I am not condoning what he did, but one would have to be in his shoes to understand his thought process. Remember he was an immigrant that came to Canada with nothing and so far has had a long full life. I firmly believe that dad picking him up once we got the farm added longevity to his life.

The Little Pony Tractor

We needed a variety of feed for the stock, but the grain was a mainstay for the three classes of stock we had, hogs, cattle, and roosters. Dad also had a few spots where he could go each summer and cut hay as required.

We owned a Massey Ferguson Pony tractor. Dad would cut the grass with his tractor, and after it was dried, he would windrow the dried hay into swaths. A neighbor who owned a baler would bale the hay for us. Cash never changed hands. Everyone worked together. It was an excellent time to head out to fields. Enjoying the warm sun while playing in the fields as dad was cutting the hay. The smell of fresh cut grass with alfalfa and clover had a particular smell; a scent that has stayed with me all these years.

When the hay was baled, it was time to get it home and undercover. We would head out with old blue, the neighbors truck and trailer and start loading the bales. Drive home unload at both places ours and the neighbors continue until the job was complete usually around 7 at night, then to the creek for a swim, and home for a late meal. This process would continue until we got enough to feed the cattle.

The tractor is very similar to the one we had on our little farm. Damn near lost my fingers putting the mower back in place after changing the blade. Learned do not stick fingers where they do not belong.

Smelting and Hog Mash

When we were growing up, and spring arrived on the north shore of Lake Superior, one of the highlights would be the arrival of the smelt run. This small silvery fish, about six to eight inches in length was delicious, and as long as the smelts were running, we would have a few feeds every spring from the dip net to the frying pan.

Word would travel, by mouth, from friend to friend, that is how we knew when the smelts were running. Down to the mouth of the current river with old blue, buckets and smelt dip net get set for an evening's worth of work.

We had a homemade dip net with a handle about ten to fifteen feet long. The net was about three feet in diameter about three foot deep, made from the wire from the rabbit hutch. It actually worked and did the job very well.

Once we arrived, we would get a spot on the bank of the river where we could reach out into the river and try to fill the net with fish. Sometimes it would take a long time, as the smelt run was not very thick, and other nights it seemed that each dip we could get a dip net half full. We would only catch what we would need to make a batch of Papu and dad's mash for the hogs. Dad would empty the net into the buckets, and we would carry the bucket to the truck and dump it into the bushel baskets that were sitting in the box of old blue. Once we got seven or eight baskets full that would be enough for the night.

During the smelt run, we might do this for three or four times over a 2 to 3 week period. We always stopped on the way home so we could give a small bucket of smelts to nana and papu so they could have a fresh feed of smelts. Mom would clean a few batches and freeze them for later use. We would always have a meal or two of fresh smelts during this time.

One night when we got home, we found some of the smelts were still alive, and my brother and I thought we could keep them alive put them in a pail of water. They lasted for a couple days, as we got bored with them. The smelts ended up in the hog mash including the ones we had in the buckets. Sometimes it was very late when we got home so the hog mash would not have gotten started until the next day.

The hog mash was grain boiled in a 200 hundred gallon vat sitting on concrete blocks up high enough so we could start a good-sized wood fire under the vessel. This concoction made from old produce from Uncle Nick's store, the little silvery fish, ample amount of grain that we had on hand. Then cooked for five to six hours and the hogs seemed to love it. This was Papu's job when he came to visit he enjoyed sitting by the caldron and keeping the fire going.

Sometimes when cooking the mash on weekends, after our chores were complete, we would sit by the fire with dad and papu and bake potatoes for a snack. Nothing fancy just go to the garden dig a hill of potatoes, take the biggest ones for our meal.

Mom checking her garden, on occasion found potato hills half dug up, spuds going to waste we were busted. After that, we would then clean up all the potatoes and the ones we did not want, ended up in the mash. Thought we were smart, but mom told me years later that she knew what was going on.

Once we got the spuds, we would bury them in the hot coals for half to three-quarters of an hour. Wait until the skins where brunt, very dark brown bordering on black. Then take them out wait until they cooled a bit, crack them in half add, some salt, pepper use a spoon, and eat them right out of the skin. Usually allowed to have an RC cola while we were sitting by the fire with our snack.

Then it was time to bring papu home the mash had been boiling and simmering for some hours, and it was time to allow the fire go out and let the pig swill cool down so it would be ready for feeding in the morning.

The Chicken Hook vs. Smelt Net

Summer was a busy time, we were always doing our chores, chores would be first then play time if time allowed. The dog days of summer would appear, and with that, we learned how to handle another piece of the operation the Rooster sales. We would sell the Roosters 5, 10, or even a 100 depending what the customer wanted. Well catching 5, 10 or more roosters was no easy chore. After dad's back operation, Rick and I did a lot of the running to snag a bird. Although my father was not as quick as he once was, he developed techniques where he could snag a bird, but it took a little longer. We started with a couple of 48-inch chicken catcher leg hooks, a 48-inch rod with a hook configuration on one end and wooden handle on the other. Using the hook, meant quietly as possible, sneak up on the rooster and snag his leg. Once he was caught, reach down, grab both legs and release the hook. From here, he would go into the customers sack if he wanted them alive, if not he would go to the block where dad was waiting, took the bird chopped off his head and then it would go into the customers sack after it had bled out.

It did not take long for these birds to figure out what was happening. We got our fair share of exercise chasing birds around this compound, and when they got smarter myself, Rick and Bruce would corner a few and then with two hooks on the go we would usually get 1 bird sometimes two. There we were we learned how to catch, chop the heads off if required and how to collect the money and store it in the tobacco tin. Birds sold for seventy-five cents to a dollar each.

Dad and Mom were away one afternoon in town shopping for supplies, and they left me in charge. We had a few customers come in for roosters only small amounts, so it worked out that we got them quickly. Things were going well, and then a customer came in wanted 50 birds all with the heads cut off.

So the three of us boys decided we could handle this it would make dad proud. Catching 50 birds with a hook, was a nightmare. These birds this afternoon were not cooperating, and we ran and ran, cornered them, and after about an hour, we had caught five. We had to snag 45 more. We were tired, hot, and dry with our tongues hanging out. We were not sure how this was going to work out. I thought for a moment, we need a plan and a different method for catching these dumb birds. Then the sun glistened off dads smelt dip net sitting on the outside of rooster yard. I thought this would work, chase the silly bird and drop the smelt net over the head, walk up, grab the roasters legs and off to the block, he would go. The brothers saw what I was doing and immediately said dad is going to be mad especially if we break his net. We decided we would try it. The first rooster started moving away from me, I speed up positioned the smelt net over his head and dropped it, boom we got him, Ricky tried, and it worked for him too. Bruce would bring the bird to the block, and that would be the end of him. We caught the remaining roosters in an hour or so and sent the customer on his way. Dad was proud when he found out that we sold that many roosters. Just after he came home and things were settled down a bit a new customer showed up and wanted twenty birds, dad asked us to come and help we had not told him about the net method yet as we thought we would fill him in when the time is right. The hooks were retrieved and handed to Rick and me, away we went after catching a couple of birds, Ricky and I looked at each other and decided now would be the time for a change, we wouldn't tell him, just show him. He wanted to know what and where was I going. Rick was still running around with the hook trying to catch a rooster, I got the net and never paid any attention to what dad was saying, or asking. Just went about my business trying to grab a silly bird and the dip net trick worked we had caught one, Rick came over and brought the bird to dad, in half an hour the job was complete. Dad said a great job, but we are going to have to modify the net make it lighter and easier to use. We finished the task, dad was smiling, and we sat down on the dirt in the hot sun and shared an RC Cola.

Growing up on the farm 1960 to 1965

Growing up on the farm with our cat 1960 to 1965

"Tony's Joe" First Communion in 1957

Ricky's First Communion in 1959

Bruce's First Communion in 1961

Politicians Brains and Ethics?

The death of a national dream came about when the government of the day turned on its own people from my perspective and canceled the Avro Arrow project. The story of the arrow is a sad one. This project was putting Canada on the map leading us into a new world, a leader, along with a few other nations building a top of the line supersonic jet, a high-speed interceptor that could do near Mach 2 speeds at 50,000 feet. This aircraft would make Canada a leader in the aviation industry. I do not think at the time the conservatives and John Diefenbaker campaigned on the idea of scrapping the Arrow project. An idea that would kill a fledgling industry in Canada. This would have put us on the world stage. The arrow was by far, ahead of anything on the market. We were developing a superb fighter jet as well as a new high-tech industry in Canada. In 1957 the first prototype was introduced to rave reviews, the government of the day was investing money in this project and was looking forward to the day when all Canadians would be proud of this investment would produce long-term high tech jobs for Canadians. With a new government, led by a man with a prickly nature and a party that firmly believed that the government should not be helping the private industry grow using government money even though it would be a great thing for our country. The government canceled the Avro Arrow project on February 20, 1959. This direction from the conservatives immediately halted the development of the Arrow and its Iroquois engines. Two months later, the government of the day, the Conservatives, and their leader John Diefenbaker ordered the assembly line, tooling, plans and any aircraft that existed destroyed. This position terminated 14,528 Avro employees, and another 15,000 supply chain employees lost their jobs. A hell of a way to have 30,000 people not have to carry a lunch bucket. It started as Black Friday, as far as I am concerned, and it is only my opinion that this set the country back and I feel we still have not recovered. February 20, 1959, was know as Black Friday the day a national dream died. Our aviation industry personnel left the country to go and work in other parts of the world in the airline sector. Some say the government killed the project to appease our neighbor's to the South, who feared they would lose prestige and sales to their northern neighbor. Had this direction, not been taken, I often wonder where our country would be today.

Photo From casmuseum.techno-science.ca

End of My 1st Decade

The winter came, we were in the new house, and life settled down. Back in school and a new decade beginning the 50's were over now we were going into the sixties.

In the late 50's the political scene in Canada was changing. Lester B Person who won a Nobel Peace prize for a satisfactory resolution to the Suez Canal crisis became the leader of the Liberal Party of Canada after Louis St Laurent resigned; he lost the election to John Diefenbaker a lawyer and a conservative from Saskatchewan. Diefenbaker won a minority government in 57; in 1958, he called a snap election after only one year in power. Dief, the Chief, his nickname, felt the conservatives needed a majority government to carry out his mandate. Diefenbaker's Conservatives won a massive majority crushing the liberals, which gave him the authority to govern the country how he saw fit.

He was supposed to be the Prime Minister for the average person, to this day I am still trying to figure out what that exactly means. It seems that no matter who gets in power, the political party comes first and the average person comes in second. The candidates during an election tell us all about the change we would like to see, they get our vote, then for the next four years or so we are history. What did this have to do with my life well Dad thought this man (Diefenbaker) was going to make it better for all of us? The story I remember dad thinking he was going to get his job back on the railway, the man promised good times the average person will not have to carry a lunch bucket, I will lead you to the Promised Land.

I did not realize it then, but this helped develop my cynical nature towards politicians.

In 1959 another Conservative leader Stephen Harper was born. Jacques Plante became the first goalie in the National Hockey League to wear a protective facemask.

Tommy Douglas was still leading the province of Saskatchewan, and Ernest Manning won his seventh consecutive majority in Alberta provincial politics.

At the end of the decade, I was nine years old; left my secure neighborhood moved to the country learned a multitude of things. The innocence of childhood disappeared fast. As I grew older work, more prevalent in our daily lives, but there was playtime when time permitted, it was always good to see Raymond's Joe coming out for a visit, or going to Little Italy to see him. This provided a necessary break in an otherwise very regimented life. By the end of 1959, a new house was $13,000, a liter of gas was .06 cents, a loaf of bread was .22 cents, and a kilogram of hamburger was 0.99 cents or 0.45 cents per lb. A 10lb box of lutefisk was around $3.00 just in case anyone is interested and the average wage for a working person was about $5,000 per year.

Thinking back now, I never knew where the money came from.

We had a car, old blue, Massey Ferguson pony tractor, and we moved into a new home, with a brand new television. So being a nosey child, I asked, and dad explained some of the in and outs of the farm. I knew we made some money selling the stock just not how much.

Doing a bit of research on what we sold in a year back in 1960 dad grossed about 6,000 dollars in a year. What we netted was just enough to survive on. During this time frame, Dad also bid on a contract to trim road edges in the municipality. Each year we got a little older which meant the more chores we could handle. I learned in later years that dad was quite a gambler. As I sit here writing this, thinking of an earlier time, I wondered if dad gambled when we were on the farm. Never did ask him about it, just seemed that some days we had more cash than others.

1960 A New Decade

Nineteen sixty rolled in and we started a new decade. I was finishing grade 3 for the second time; it was okay but I was learning to love the farm a little more each year, I felt comfortable here often wondered how long would I have to go to school. Mom and dad kept repeating themselves you will finish high school, that would be a significant accomplishment for our family as mom and dad only had grade 8 as far as I could remember. My brother Ricky was in grade two, Brucey was still at home. Summer came around, education, over for the year, and I was looking forward to grade four. We were happy; we were not rich by monetary standards but well off with love and happiness in our home and family. I learned how to appreciate the good things in life as well as the material things. Having clothes and other products handed down was not a downer that was life; the goods were new to me, so it did not matter where they came from. I remember my first ball glove black in color, were it came from I do not know, it was not a brand new glove, it was passed onto me, it was great, now I could play ball at school.

The next four years on the farm, my brothers and I spent time doing a multitude of tasks. We had our daily chores to do which included milking old Betsy, cleaning the barn, feeding the hogs and roosters as well as selling the damn birds on occasion. The summers are especially enjoyable as we helped with hay, boxcar cleaning and then we had the garden to weed. The brothers and I found time to be kids, swimming, fishing, even though there was always work to be done. Mom was pregnant in the winter of 59/60, and we knew that our lives were going to change again. My brothers and I, not sure how, but we knew it was going to involve some drastic changes and bring on more work. Oh well, such is life, a term that gets repeatedly used by many people. On August 6, 1960, mom had a baby. The baby was a little girl named Charlotte Ann, mom and dad's little princess she became. I knew from the moment she came home we were in trouble. She was the best thing that happened in 1960 according to mom and dad; I thought that when we got bikes in the spring of 60 that was the best thing.

In the spring of 60, we got a surprise one day. Dad came home and had bikes for us. They were not new, but we were excited nonetheless. We were getting freedom handed to us on two wheels. My bike was a used balloon tired streamliner, single speed. It was phenomenal.

Photo From schwinncruisers.com similar to the second-hand bike I received back in the late 50's or early 60's

There was an alternative reason that I figured out well writing this. When we took the bus, we would leave early about 8:30, and we wouldn't get home as the bus went in reverse till about 5:00. Dad figured if we took our bikes to school we could leave a little later in the morning but be home a lot earlier in the evening which resulted in more time for chores. Worked for him, worked for me. Pedaling down the road, wind blowing through my hair freedom, well it was remarkable. We could go home for lunch some days which was great. Other days we would get a nickel or a dime to stop at the store on the bottom of John Sreet Road. We could go in and get 15 licorice kids for a nickel. On a special day, we received a dime we could get candy and a bag of chips. Life was simple, but in fact, it was grand. It was surprising how much that bike meant to me; indeed it did give me the freedom that I never knew existed.

An Adventure Speckled Trout Fishing

At this stage in life, dad was not much of a fisherman, or he just didn't have the time to do it, or the inclination of walking up and down a creek through the bramble bushes for a fish didn't seem to suit is style. Not to say dad didn't like the outdoors he was more of a hunter. In the fall of the year, dad and his compadres would go moose hunting, some years they were lucky, and they would get one or two moose, its funny with all the meat we had on the farm there was always moose meat in the freezer.

Dad skinning a moose in the old garage on the farm. He loved his moose meat.

[109]

Mr. Ward, a neighbor who lived a couple of doors away from us, was a fisherman. I remember seeing Mr. Ward coming back from fishing on Saturdays, one day on his way home, I was on the front lawn when Mr. Ward asked me if I would like to see his catch. Being inquisitive I said yes, and he showed the trout that he had in his basket. Six speckled trout that were about 10 to 12 inches long. I asked where and how he got them. Neebing River about 5 miles up the road he said, and with that, he headed home. I thought about the fish that he had caught thought it was neat, but they would probably smell when they were cooked, although the smelt, were fish the way mom cooked them there was no lutefisk smell, that smell would always be associated with fish.

He came over on occasion to visit with mom and dad and noticed that I had a new bike. "Well, young fella, with that beautiful looking bike, you will be able to come fishing with me on Saturday, if it is okay with your dad," I was looking at Mr. Ward too and thanked him for the offer and explained that I didn't have a rod or reel. This will not be a problem I am sure I can fix you up with one. It was happening again someone offering to give me something free of charge, and it would make my life better. I am learning quickly that the neighbors on the farm are just like my family in Little Italy warm, loving and gracious.

Now with a new bike, I had an offer to go on a new adventure as long as I could get dads permission. "Dad Mr. Ward asked me to go fishing with him on Saturday do you think it will be alright if I go." There was silence for a while and dad finally spoke: "I can't see any problem as long as your chores are done before you go, and when you get home do not forget about the evening chores." I got the answer I was hoping for and went directly over to Mr. Wards to give him the news. "Dad said yes, I could go fishing with you, what do I need." "You will need lunch and something to drink, I will take care of everything else we will leave the house at 7:00. Can you come over tomorrow night and we will dig up some worms for bait." "Sure will see you in the evening," I said as I drove out the driveway excited as can be.

Three sleeps before I could embark on this adventure. The next night after chores and school work complete headed over to Mr. Wards and he showed me how to dig for worms the bait we would require. Before I left, he gave me a package to take home it was all in a packsack. He told me I could use to carry my lunch and drinks for our quest. I got home showed mom and dad inside there was a three piece rod, reel, and a fishing kit with the necessary hooks and sinkers, I thought it was Christmas.

Friday evening finally came one more sleep and off on the quest to catch fish. I did all my chores that night plus whatever I could get done any other jobs so I could lessen my load the next morning. Got in the house mom helped me make my lunch and stored it in the refrigerator. Off to bed, I went thinking I won't get any sleep tonight but before long I was out like a light.

The alarm clock made a hell of a racket at 5:30 in the morning. Up and dressed, outdid my chores in record time. Back into the house gulped down some breakfast, Mom and Dad were up, mom made me a thermos of coffee kissed them goodbye, grabbed my gear and out the door I went. Jumped on my bike and meet Mr. Ward and we proceeded to go for a ride to the fishing hole.

After a half hour leisurely ride we made it to Neebing River and parked our bikes in the bush where they would not be seen. Then off to the creek, we walked for about 5 minutes, and we were at the start of the fishing holes. Mr. Ward explained that we were going to fish the pools and around deadfalls, the first pool we encountered also had a significant deadfall in so he was able to show me what the fishing holes looked like. When fishing Mr. Ward said you have to be patient, this is a patient man's game. I did not know what to expect, but within a half hour, I knew what he was talking about. The first 60 minutes I spent just watching and learning.

Neebing River hasn't changed too much used to park our bikes in the bush on the left-hand side so they could not be seen from the road.

First Mr. Ward taught me how to bait the hook. That worm sure didn't want to get stuck on that hook as he squiggled and tried to get away. Then he showed me how to get the line with a hook and worm out into the pond and how to work it. Before long Mr. Ward was explaining what the line would be doing when a trout was coming in for a bite. Then when the fish was biting, he taught me how to set the hook, with a quick wrist action just lifting the tip of the rod holding the line taut, this would set the hook. Then you have a little fight on your hands as you try and get the fish close to you so you can catch him, take fishhook out and put him in your bag or basket.

After watching for the 30 minutes, we moved on to another pool, and Mr. Ward told me it was my turn. He watched me bait the hook, and after a few times that part of the job was done, that worm was a slimy little burger. Then out into the pond, the hook and worm went, after working the line back and forth to no avail, nothing was happening. Then I remembered what Mr. Ward said about being patient. So I kept on going and doing what he taught me to do. The more I practiced, the more comfortable I got with using the rod and reel. I checked my hook out, and it required some new bait as the old worm had fallen off.

I rebated my hook and cast my line out to the center and was slowly working the line when I felt something, at least thought I did. Cast out again the same area, and as I was winding in I definitely felt a bite, or so I thought. Mr. Ward was watching me and told me cast in the same spot but retrieve the hook slower. My heart was pounding with anticipation. As I was winding the hook in something grabbed my hook and bent my rod in half. I almost let it go, "Mr. Ward what's happening" I screeched, "you got one," he said, "wind him in" so very carefully started reeling him in got him up on the river bank, "beautiful fish," Mr. Ward said about 10 inches long. I was smiling from ear to ear what a blast that was I have never had so much fun. We continued up and down the creek crossing where we could and fishing all pools and deadfalls. After about three hours we had six fish each, and Mr. Ward thought that was enough. He then suggested that we have a bite to eat beside the creek before we made it back to our bikes. This was a great adventure. We sat down to open up our packs and took out a sandwich, then I opened up my thermos and poured a cup of coffee. I asked Mr. Ward if he wanted a cup coffee and said no thanks he preferred tea. I like my coffee with 3 sugars still do to this day. I have never tasted anything like that sandwich and coffee or was it the ambiance that made it so great. As we were finishing up our lunch, Mr. Ward complemented me on my first day of fishing and said anytime I could go I was welcome to come with him. I thanked him very much.

We were putting our stuff in our backpacks when we heard a loud woof from across the creek. I looked up, and my eyes got as big as saucers, a giant black bear was looking at us. Mr. Ward said get up slowly grab your backpack and start moving backward very slowly and get behind me. As we were doing this, the bear stood up on his hind legs and let out a roar that drained the blood from my face, Mr. Ward looked at me and said I was as white as a ghost. That growl scared the crap out of me, I thought I am going to drop everything and run like hell. Mr. Ward said keep backing up, so I did as I was told. The bear was still on the other side of the river, at first I thought we were going to be his lunch, but we got onto the pathway and then slowly turned and walked back to our bikes. The bear stayed on his side of the river. We got to our bikes about an hour later loaded up and pedaled for home.

Home again said thank you to Mr. Ward for taking me. It was time to show the fish to mom and dad, fill them in on the day, the fishing, the bear and anything in between. Mom cleaned the fish, and we had them for supper no lutefisk smell the best fish I've ever eaten in my early life. There was a bounce in my step, what a day, what an adventure, did my chores and I hardly knew I was doing any work. The next four years Mr. Ward and I went fishing a few more times. Days we caught lots of fish and other days never got any. These trips taught me a lot about patience and stamina that carried with me so throughout my life. This first venture was grand, and will always be embedded in my memory.

A Sister

On August 6, 1960, Charlotte Ann was born. Our family consisted of three boys and one new sister. Mom, Dad, and the rest of our family, immediate and extended, thought she was special. Mom and dad thought they had a little princess on their hands. As she got older, she figured the princesses scenario out and used it to her full advantage. It was a good thing we had the new house. There was no way we would have fit into the old tarpaper shack. We were growing like bad weeds Papu would say, the wholesome food and clean air contributed to a healthy lifestyle. The old place was getting tight, as space was limited, although we could have turned the living room into a nursery if we had to. The new house was a far better option.

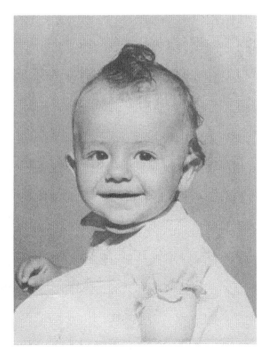

Dads princess three months old

With this new kid in the picture, the household dynamic was changing. Brucey would be going to school in the fall. He was growing up and would start being a help instead of a hindrance. The chores now split three ways, as Brucey and Ricky were getting older. Although I felt the lion's share still belonged to me, I was the oldest.

Now with this new kid being added to the mix and I was the oldest, babysitting was added to my repertoire of duties. This was no easy task as Brucey and Ricky could be a real pain in the ass when this new kid needed changing or she was just upset. I thought to myself when I get married someday, not sure kids would be in the picture.

Instantly the new bundle of joy changed my life. Learning in short order that being the oldest child had its benefits, but it also had many drawbacks. There just never seemed to be an abundance of time just to be a kid, do not get me wrong there was some time available just not enough. My day started with the morning chores. Feed, water, the stock with dads help, and milk the cow on occasion. Then back to the house, clean up for school, have breakfast jump on my bike or catch the bus depending on the time of the year head for a day in school. Then back home afternoon chores, supper, dishes, homework and help with the princess when required. I could not figure out why dad did not have to change diapers, and I did must have been that oldest kid scenario, there were days I was not happy with it, but I also knew enough to grin and bear it. As the next four years crept by, she got older as we all did, but not only did she have her brothers wrapped around her finger she had a lot of control over mom and dad. There were occasions when mom or dad called Charlotte Ann in an aggravated voice, we knew it was time to head to the hills because just as sure as the sun shone mostly every day she would explain it was one of the brothers that caused the problem, whoever was closest would be catching flack. She really did dominate for some years. When something did not go Charlotte's way it was our fault, and somehow trouble came our way, but we loved her even more.

Dad and his princess on the hood of old blue.

Dads princess the year before we left the farm.

Brucey and the Boar

Not sure if it was the summer of 62 or 63, but there was a day when things just did not go according to plan. It was a Saturday and had been rainy for a few days, but on this particular Saturday, the sun was shining, and it is a warm morning. With the rain that we had the ditches on both sides of John Street were full of water and mud. Much like when mom got old blue stuck in the mud when she was taking diving lessons. Brucey and Charlotte happened to be on the deck, playing with their toys, mom was in the garden, and Papu came to the farm for the day. He checked out the garden, no weeds in sight the rows clean and straight, met with his satisfaction, made mom happy. Dad, Ricky and I finished unloading the sweepings from the boxcar's and Papu who was wandering, looking and checking on who knows what when he told Dad "get the vat ready we are low on mash." Dad had other jobs that he wanted to be done today; he figured it would not take long to get the hog food ready. Getting the pig food ready would give Papu a job for the day. We added the grain, water and the other fixings, started the fire. The new batch of mash was on its way to being cooked, and Papu was happy.

We had a boar that dad figured was too unpredictable to have on the farm; he was always kicking up a fuss or trying to get out of the hog pen. Dad decided we needed some fresh pork for Papa, Nana's freezer, and ours. The whole time we lived on the farm dad provided Nana and Papa with meat. I always thought that was a neat way of taking care of his parents, I am sure that they helped him out somehow when we got the farm, my speculation anyway. Dad asked me to help him put the stock crate in old blue. This was a homemade container, but it did the job. When loaded on the truck the ramp would tilt down allow the stock to get up into the stock carrier on old blue, then lift the ramp lock in place close tailgate and you are on your way. Dad would then transport the animals to the auction or maybe the meat packing plant. We had the crate loaded on the truck, time put the plan into action, load this pig, and send him on his way.

Dad called mom from the garden, she ventured up to the farmyard to see what we needed. There were the four of us this should not be too difficult. Dad explained the plan; open the gate, back old blue into position, drop the ramp, close the gates, so they were snug on the edge of the ramp. This way the boar would have no option except to go up the ramp into the crate. Therefore all we had to do was coral that hog, chase him up the ramp, close lift the ramp lock it in place, lift the tailgate pull the old blue out shut the gate, and we'll be on our way. Should not take more than 15 minutes. That was the plan.
The pigpen was muddy and slippery, we all had rubber boots (shit stickers) on, and Papu came over to the fence to watch the commotion. Well, the plan was coral the boar, then close in on him, and force him up the ramp. The idea was working then this shithead pig decided no I am not doing this, spun around and broke through our human shield. Brushed by me catching me on the leg and knocked me ass over teakettle into the mud. I got up stammering and said "SHIT," Dad looked at me and said watch your language, I had a few more superlatives that I kept under my breath. That hog just pissed me off, and I thought to myself, you will be pork chops soon, not fast enough for me. The whole time this was going on Papu and dad were jabbering in Italian and Papu was laughing, he thought this was quite a site. We took a break while

dad decided the next plan of action would be. Dad went and got the cattle prods a little electric shock would get him moving in the right direction. This dam hog weighed between two and three hundred lbs and was about 3 feet high from the back to the ground. We circled around him and started to move him back to the ramp. Poking him with prods, he knew he did not want to come back towards us. I thought, yes we got him this time. He was moving slowly towards the ramp dad said "do not rush him," we slowed a bit, and the hog was at the base of the ramp, sniffing around not sure what he was going to do. Then the unbelievable happened, I watched this hog, he put his snout under the ramp, and he lifted, and the ramp moved, I thought, crap he is going to escape. Dad said Joe "give him a shot in the ass with the prod get him going up the ramp." We all closed in, and Papu let out a shriek, I prodded him, and before we knew it, the ramp went up, and that damn hog squeezed out between the tire and the gate. There was no way that I figured he would fit, he proved me wrong he was out. Papu yelling in Italian. He was going to try to stop him; Papu was over 80 now dad yelled at Papu, "Dad stop" in Italian "let him go." This dam pig was meandering down the driveway at a good clip. I hoped over the fence with Rick in tow. Mom and dad following, we were all heading down the road yelling and hollering trying to get this stupid pig to stop. Papu decided to stay up by the fire pit thank goodness.

I looked up, Brucey heard all the commotion and decided he was going to come and help, he ran out to the middle of the driveway making a racket using his little boy voice trying to make it loud and threatening with his arm waving in the happening this large animal would stop. However, the boar kept bearing down on him. The pig had its head low to the

[122]

ground, the next thing I saw, I could not believe my eyes. The head went between Bruce's legs, this poor little gaffer, tears starting to flow riding this pig backward calling for mom and dad to help. The look on his face and the color he turned was something to see, now I understood that Mr. Ward meant when he said I looked like a ghost when we ran into the bear.

Bruce was as white as a newborn lamb, hung on for dear life, to what I do not know, rode that hog right across the road and down into the ditch. Once into the mud, the pig stopped abruptly, and Brucey fell off into the mud, came up sputtering and spitting water out his mouth. He got his bearing and shot out of that ditch into mom's arms, he was not sure if he should cry or laugh I think he did a little of both.

After I had realized he was okay I started to laugh, he was not happy with that and came after me with arms flailing, I put my hand on his head and said quit that, or I will throw you back in that mud beside the pig. Mom then said, "Joey stop laughing and leave him alone." With all the commotion that was going on the neighbors showed up, Dad brought old blue down and got it set so we could load this hog. With the friend's help, we got the damn pig onto the truck. Dad thanked neighbors for their support, now he could finally be on his way to get rid of this shithead pig. The job that was only going to take fifteen minutes to do burned up a good portion of the day.

We all went back into the yard after dad left and I was going to go to the house to change clothes. When mom spotted this, "stop," she shrieked, "You are not going in like that come over here by the hose." Begrudgingly, Brucey and I moseyed on to where mom had the hose, and she rinsed all the mud off our clothes. To the basement with you, strip, change

[123]

clothes, and then back out here so we can finish the chores. The princess in the meantime continued playing on the deck with her toys oblivious to what was going.

Dad delivered that hog, and when he came home, a short time later with the empty truck, I knew that pig was gone for good.

We finished the chores dad my brothers and me; dad then figured it was time for a snack, grabbed some spuds from the garden and cooked them just the way we liked them. Thinking about the day, I started to chuckle, and Brucey even got a smile on his face.

Dad was telling Papu what had happened once the hog got down in the ditch on the other side of the road with Brucey, and I could see Papu smiling and then he was laughing, a Walter Brenan type of laugh deep from the stomach and full of life.

We ate our snacks talked and laughed the rest of the day away, what an adventure. The fire dying down Dad took Papu home. Chores were complete, down to the house we went helped mom and then sat and watched hockey night in Canada. The boar well in a couple of weeks we had fresh pork chops and bacon, it brought a smile to my face, that will teach you for knocking me into the mud. Life was beautiful.

*Brucey around 1962/1963 at the time he went for a
ride on the boar.*

Christmas on the Farm

Christmas, on the farm, was a festive time. We were always going somewhere, could have been a visit with Grandpa and Grandma. Or going to the annual Christmas sock party complete with lutefisk at Grandpas and Grandma's. To Uncle Nicks store on Ontario Street or visiting with Nana and Papu on Christmas Day after Mass. There was always cookies and Mandarin oranges from the Far East. They came in the neatest little wooden boxes, usually about 5 lbs, not what we get today; you did not have to have a bankroll to buy them.

Christmas started for mom and dad in November sometime. Mom would try to get gifts for us and hide them. Many of the presents came from Simpson Sears and Eatons. The other thing was, baking, and by the time Christmas arrived, there was Chinese chews, shortbread, dark fruitcakes and a multitude of other sweets that we could have. So besides the baking and other foods that were prepared for the big day. There was an evening set aside for us kids to go and do our shopping. Each one of us would have to purchase five gifts, one for mom and dad, the brothers and our sister the princess.

We received ten to twenty dollars each to do our shopping depending on the year; it always coincided with dad selling a few more piglets. He kept a few hogs, throughout the summer, letting them grow until they reached market size, a couple of hundred lbs, and then sold them in mid-December, these were the Christmas hogs. We were on winter break from school so our excursion would be set up for Friday night a week or two before Christmas. We had to get the chores done early so we could leave by five o'clock the stores were only open until nine o'clock, so we had to have a plan. We would have a draw to see which one of us was going to get dad the old spice shaving kit it had the shaving bowl full of soap, a brush to put soap on your face as well as a bottle of old spice shaving lotion. If we did not have the draw dad would get three or four shaving kits for Christmas. Funny when I smell old spice it brings a memory of a real happy time when twenty dollars, could buy everyone a gift. Ready to go, pile into the car, plan in place, chores complete, dad would drop us downtown Thunder Bay North around Red River Road and Court Street, then he would head to Nanas and Papu's for a visit with them and Uncle Nicky.

There we were standing in amongst the crowd eyes wide open, the country bumpkins coming into town to their Christmas shopping. It was as if we had never seen this skeptical before. Christmas was always a magical time, window displays; the streets decorated with lights, stores playing Christmas music and people all over hustling and bustling trying to find that perfect gift.

Ricky and I could wander off ahead of mom, Brucey, and Charlotte, as long as we did not get too far ahead. The stores were all loaded with goodies and gifts, most stores had lunch counters at the time you could shop and get a bite to eat with a drink, would defiantly be well under two dollars. One thing I remember is the floors in these old five and dime stores they were hardwood. Just like the floors, we had in our old house on the farm. They were never level there seemed to be indistinct rolls and squeaks on the floor. This added to the character of the building and the shopping experience. We would be dressed in our winter grab just like everyone else. It was usually cold on these excursions, but we enjoyed every moment.

Everywhere you looked, there was merchandise. The stores all brought in extra, and it was hard to move around, as there were people everywhere. Sometimes it was a snowy evening, and that would add to the ambiance of the adventure. In one store, buy a pair of gloves, off to another shop for old spice shaving kit. This calamity continued until each one of us finished our shopping. Each had five gifts to purchase with their twenty dollars. They could be socks, ties, scarves; comb sets whatever would strike our fancy. As we went from store to store, each store had its own lunch counter with the aroma of their favorite specialty. We had to pick a store with a lunch counter, this is how the evening ended eating out, and we thought we were kings. What a fantastic treat. Sitting at the lunch counter ordering up a burger, fries with gravy and pop. Still, to this day, I enjoy a burger, fries, and gravy at some backwoods greasy spoon. A memory I will always have.

After eating we would go out and wait for dad, said he would pick us up where he dropped us, shortly after nine. The magical lights and the Christmas music, slowly fading out. A remarkable sight, a memory that I have cherished throughout my life. The downtown was slowly going to sleep, watching this I guess we were really country bumpkins.

I remember a Christmas we got a gift that was for my brothers and myself, a record player. It was from Santa, with younger brothers and sister Santa lived a long life at our house. This record player was small, new technology, it was about 1 ft.^{2} and maybe 4 inches high, electric, it could play long play albums and 45's. It was either 62 or 63 when Santa delivered this to us; we got three long play albums with this gift. The records that we received were Bobby Vinton's Blue Velvet, The Best of Johnny Horton and Marty Robbins, Gunfighter Ballads and Trail Songs. We wore these albums out after playing them repeatedly.

I enjoyed getting presents, but at the same time, I also enjoyed watching everyone open his or her unique gifts on Christmas morning. This was outstanding time; we got off the farm for the evening and went out, going out on this particular adventure. It was a night that we could look at the world filled with wonder and awe at this fantastic time of the year. This time prepared me for life-learning lessons; the joys of giving will always be with me whether it was gifts, knowledge or just companionship. This would without exception, always bring a smile to someone's face.

One of the many Christmas on the farm. Front Brucey making faces, left Rickey, Charlotte the Princess, and "Tony's Joe." Many happy memories.

A Few Family Highlights

Although the first half of the decade was humdrum, it did have its highlights and drawbacks. In 1962, Papu and Nana celebrated their 60th wedding anniversary. A challenge, this remarkable achievement, spanned two continents, six decades, two world wars and a lot of hard work. Papu and Nana were 80 and 76 years old respectively. There was a massive celebration at the Italian Hall celebrating this event with all kind of local dignitary's attending with a multitude of family and friends. The meal consisted of spaghetti and meatballs, salads, more pop that I have ever seen in my life in fact more of anything that I had ever seen in my life. There was dancing with a live band, and fun for all, we even snuck down into the games room but were quickly ushered out and back up to the main party. Throughout my time in Thunder Bay, I attended many celebrations in the Italian Hall. There were weddings, funerals, and other get-togethers, but this was my first gala that I remembered, what a grand party.

Family Picture is taken at Italian Hall Nana's and Papu's 60ᵗʰ wedding anniversary

Nana and Papu's 60ᵗʰ wedding anniversary

Turmoil at Home and In the World

After two world wars, and then the Korean conflict, one would have thought the world would have settled down by now. Not to be the Americans, the Russians, Chinese, and other countries got involved in the Vietnam conflict. Still no peace. Throughout the 60's, the world as we knew it, was full of turmoil. People could not or did not want to coexist together. We seemed to be a world full of hate, just trying our damn'st, to destroy the world, mankind along with it.

The first half, the cold war was in full swing, Russia and the United States just could not get along. With both country's possessing nuclear weapons and there was constant saber rattling about who was going to use them first. In October, of 1962, the Russians decided they were going to station nuclear missiles on the island of Cuba.

This created a world of unknowns, would these two countries go to war, and annihilate the world. No one new but everyone was scared. Air raid sirens were placed at strategic points around the cities and in the schools to warn people of impending doom. Expectations were that people take shelter if the sirens went off at designated locations. Thank goodness, it never came to that. Cooler heads prevailed, but the world, as, we knew it changed; we would always have that terrible threat hanging over us. In 1947, the development of the doomsday clock; was created to let everyone know how close we were to global annihilation. If it ever hits 12:00 midnight, God help us all, as humanity, could be annihilated.

The government of John Diefenbaker was in hot water with the Americans because he would not put our troops on full alert during this crisis.

Then the word was in a constant state of flux. The news of the assassination of John Fitzgerald Kennedy on November 22, 1963, rocked the world. Schools closed for the day, we were sent home to spend the time with our parents. Part of the world mourned this loss while other factions rejoiced; he was just too liberal for his country as well as many other nations. We all wondered from the youngest to the oldest what was going to happen now. These times just continued to be scary times. We were a close family thank goodness; we had each other to hang onto throughout these turbulent times.

In our great country, Saskatchewan launched the first Medicare plan on July 1, 1962. The doctors of the time were dead against this project, and they protested to show their displeasure. Where, would we be today, without some forward thinking individuals at this time? They had the guts and the fortitude to bring Medicare about.

In 1964, Lester B Pearson became prime minister of Canada defeating John Diefenbaker. I like to think that the problems with the Americans and the Avro Arrow debacle helped boot him and the conservative party out of power.

Hockey in time, with the birth of Wayne Gretzky in 1961 would change forever; he would have a profound effect on the game. This would come about as long as we could keep the politician's fingers in their pockets, and not on the red button to destroy the world.

Up to now, my life had its ups and down's, mostly up's, and for the last little while it was going smoothly, even with all the scares about the world ending. I was heading to my 15th birthday. In the spring of 1965, times were changing my world would be rocked again. The CNR decided that they had a job for dad; this would get him off the books as an injured worker. It was not much of a job. Dad would clean the passenger cars that traveled from Thunder Bay to Winnipeg and Sault Lookout. This meant that father could no longer sweep the boxcars, what would we do for feed; the cost to buy feed on the open market, would be too expensive, and dad wouldn't have the time to work the farm.

Uncle Nicky and Dad were discussing options it seemed Uncle Nicky was the businessman in the family, he was into the stock markets, real estate, and he appeared to know what he was doing. He had a store on Algonquin Avenue in Thunder Bay North that he had built a few years back. At this time, the store was being rented out as Uncle Nick was having a hard time working both of his stores. When Uncle Nick started the store on Algonquin Avenue, he built the business from scratch. I listened and figured out, part of the conversation, Dad and Uncle Nick were having, was for dad to take over the store on Algonquin Avenue.

So sitting here, on the farm with a long face, wondering, what would we do? I was finishing grade eight-maybe dad could work on the railway, and I could stay home and work the farm. I was going to be 15 in the fall almost a man. What would we do? Ricky was 13, Brucey was 11, Charlotte was six, and mom was pregnant. We had our lives set the cousins were back. Holy Cross turned out to be a good school, I had a plan, and Dad taught me how to plan. Life was still grand, but what was coming around the corner, I was not sure. I felt we had to stay on the farm; I felt that with all the work that I had done, this place also belonged to me.

Part 4
Back To City

The Store and High school

I should have guessed that something was up in the spring of 65. Dad sold the stock in the early spring. The season purchase of rooster chicks did not happen. We did not go to any auctions to replenish what we sold. Old Blue did not make its daily trek to the rail yard to pick up the swept grain. The yard and barn were spruced up no garden was planted. Some strange people were coming for visits all the time. They would wander all over ask a million questions, then leave. Some would come back for a second visit, there was one person who came back, was this, his fourth or fifth time, not sure. This time though he was coming in for coffee, Dad told us to go outside and play for a while. We did. There were fewer and fewer chores to do, and Papu no longer came out for the daily visits. I had a feeling this was the end of our farm life. I peeked in the window and watched as Dad and the stranger signed the papers. In the time it took to sign their names, the farm now changed hands.

Mom and Dad called us in. We have some excellent news for you kids we have sold the farm. I felt a choking sensation in my throat as a tear worked its way to the corner of my eye on hearing the news. Mom and dad continued with their story. We are buying Uncle Nicks store on Algonquin Avenue, not too far from here. Roughly knew, where it was because mom and dad took some strange ways home when we were out for a ride or visit lately. Usually, after, we passed the building there was always a quiet conversation between mom and dad. Uncle Nick told mom and dad he was going to sell the store if they were not interested then he would sell to someone else. The renter had given notice that he wanted to leave. Consequently, mom and dad accepted the deal from Uncle Nick and they purchased the building and the lot that was next to the building.

I thought that maybe this would be a good thing. I was starting high school; perhaps the workload would be more manageable. I did not believe that even for a second; it was going to be a busy time. I knew there be no more fishing with Mr. Ward, no swimming in the creek, the Saturday night shinny game at Raymond's Joe's house would disappear. Oh well, we were getting older, time to really start earning our keep, even though we did it all along, this was going to be different.

I asked dad if I could go and tell the news to Raymond's Joe. Sure, go right ahead. Thought I could grab a famous burger from Aunty Teresa at the same time. Told Raymond's Joe the news he was happy for me, he said, "come on Joe beats shoveling pig shit." He had a valid point, from Little Italy to country bumpkins back to city slickers. Sitting at the counter with Joe, Aunty T brought us a burger, I asked if she had heard the news, of course, she did, Papu and the family all gave their blessing. I realized this would have not happened without the family helping with the decision. This was the family way. What a burger we had smothered in homemade marinara sauce with melted cheese. Ate quietly, pondering on the next steps whatever they might be.

The Store - Anticipation and First Look

Dad had a big black Chrysler New Yorker station wagon. Not new, bought it second hand from a dealership where he had a good friend working. This fellow was always on the lookout for something snazzy for dad. I learned if possible do not buy new off the lot, dad claimed as soon as you sign the papers and drive off the lot you just lost at least 30% of what you paid. He felt the crap table paid better. Dad probably paid around $3000 for the car, a new vehicle was running about $5000. It seemed every couple of years dad got a new station wagon from the same fellow, I never questioned where it came from or why. The farm was quiet now, so we loaded up the car, and we're going to head into town to see our new home. This is where we would settle for the upcoming years while working this new venture.

We loaded the car with cleaning supplies, mops, bucket's, rags and pine sol. The vehicle now packed, the kids piled in and off to start a new adventure, what will it bring? Not sure.

Drove to the store parked in the driveway, the kid's new school was standing like a beacon of light right across the road, a 2 story building, a lot bigger than Holy Cross. Ricky would be going into grade eight again; he said he liked it so much that he wanted to do it again.

Uncle Nick arrived with the keys so we could get into the building. The building from the outside looked like a monstrosity, two stories two apartments on the top floor, the building 30 feet wide probably 80 feet long, white stucco a driveway on the side, parking for the apartments, parking in the front of the store. We would own the empty lot next to the store. There were apple trees 5 or 6 separating the two lots. This is the area that dad would use to park in. The door was unlocked, and Uncle Nick handed my father the key that would change our lives one more time. Ready to go in, have a look, what would we see. My face must have shown a complete lack of excitement. What I did see, a mountain of work that had our name scribbled all over it. Uncle Nick noticed this and said something to dad right away in Italian, dad looked at me and told me not to worry, his comment "hard work will bring a promising result." I never said a thing, I wanted to but thought better did not need a slap on the side of the head just yet. The place was dirty, dirtier than the pig stalls we had to clean each day. Four isle ways lots of shelving and utterly void of stock. A couple of coolers that looked okay, just a nasty mess, meat cooler, and a produce case. The size of the store thinking back would have been around 1200 to 1500 square feet could have been a bit larger who knows.

The living quarters made up the remaining square footage on this floor. This consisted of two small bedrooms, a kitchen that was a fair size, and main floor washroom. Wondered where would we sleep, down to the basement we went, we went down the stairs there was a room on our left, this would be big enough for the brothers and me. Uncle Nick and Dad were discussing building a second bedroom for the princess. Charlotte would stay upstairs until her new room was complete. The second small bedroom on the main floor would then be converted into a little living room. The baby, when born would stay in mom and dad's room at the start and then when it was older it would move down to the basement, either into the boy's room or the princess's room depending on whether it was a boy or a girl. With my luck, it would be a boy, and this little rat would invade our cramped quarters. This would be home until I left in the early 70's, sharing this room with my brothers.

Back to the main floor, we went, this was our new home, no sense in crying about. Our new house on the farm, gone, my own room was gone. Looked around, it was time to get this adventure into high gear, and all I could see was a mountain of work ahead of us. Where do we start?

The First Look at our new digs wondered what we were getting into.

Pine-Sol

After the tour of our new digs, it was time to get down, dirty, and get the cleaning party underway. This was going to be a grueling task how would we get it done. I kept thinking what Raymond's Joe had said it's better than shoveling pig shit, I knew, Raymond's Joe was right. The hardest part would be the first cleaning, after that it should be a breeze.

We unloaded the car and brought the supplies in, and the first job was to spread the dustbane on the floor to start sweeping. Not much sense in cleaning the shelves then sweeping the floor and getting dust all over everything. Dad grabbed a broom, spread the dustbane on the floor and started to clean. This material worked well and kept the dust down to a minimum.

Mom was in the back of the store where there was an oversized sink. She started filling some buckets with soapy water and a diluted mixture of pine-sol. What is Pine-Sol; to a kid it is a cleaner like no other? It has a scent that's strong, it would knock you, on your ass if you used too much. The way it smelled you really didn't want to put your hand in the bucket for fear it would take the hide right off your bones. This magic concoction that mom figured we needed would kill 99.9 percent of all germs and household bacteria on any surface as well as anything else that moved as far as I was concerned. It really was a good cleaner, and the scent was okay after a while. All the brothers and the princess had buckets, age-wise I was 14, Rick was 13, Brucey was 11, and the princess was six. Was this a catastrophe waiting to happen? My job being the tallest was the top shelf. Ricky was next then Brucey, 3 shelves three ways to clean and only one sergeant major to make sure the job passed inspection. At this time mom donned her white butcher's apron, and this became part of her wardrobe for the next 10 to 15 years while we owned the store. There were approximately 150 linear feet of shelves that required cleaning. Mom and the princess were working on some smaller areas, and once dad got the floor swept, he grabbed a bucket and started cleaning the back area. This is where the meat cooler, slicer, and butcher block where located. The store was beginning to get that pine-sol clean smell to it. We worked hard all day and then it was time to call it quits for the day.

Dad picked up some Kentucky fried chicken that we ate when we got home. A feast for all, that night, chicken, and royal crown cola, soon it would be different flavors right from our own store.

The next day being Sunday church would come first then a visit with Nana and Papu then back to our store to finish the cleaning the job. Off to church, we went, early enough so we could go to confession, confess our sins, and receive a penance, 10 Hail Mary's followed by 10 Lord's Prayer. What sins could young boys possibly have? Once we were in the confessional, something always came out. We always found something to say, we swore, used the words like pig shit or did not obey our parents. Hence the penance did not want to waste the priest's time. Said our prayers, sat quietly and listened to the priest if we misbehaved there would be hell to pay when the service was over. Church over, down to Nanas and Papu's quick visit then back to work.

We got to the store loaded our buckets with soapy water and Pine-Sol, the smell of Pine-Sol a little overwhelming now. Back to the shelves around three o'clock the shelves, walls, and coolers all complete only the floor left.

Filled up the mop buckets with soap and water and a healthy dose of Pine-Sol and proceeded to clean the floor. In an hour this was complete, the only job left, put a coat wax on the floor. Dad and mom finished the waxing while we went over to the schoolyard to horse around for a while. Came back and the store was immaculate shiny and smelled clean. Pine-Sol, a scent that is still with me some 50 years later. I associate this smell with decent, honest hard work.

Off to home we went and had our usual Sunday feast of spaghetti, meatballs, Italian sausage, covered in mom's homemade Italian spaghetti sauce, what a great weekend the new adventure well under way.

Meat Ball Recipe

1lb lean ground burger
1lb ground pork
1lb ground chicken (optional)
10 eggs
1-cup Romano Parmesan or Parmigiano-Reggiano cheese
1-cup plain breadcrumbs
2 tablespoons garlic powder
4 tablespoons onion powder
2 teaspoons salt
3 teaspoons black pepper
1-tablespoon oregano leaves

Place all spices in a bowl whisk together
Place all meat in a large mixing bowl
Add eggs cheese breadcrumbs work until mixed
Add spices mix with hands until sticky and able to form the required meatball size.
Once you reach the required consistency, let sit for 1 to 2 hours in the refrigerator to allow spices to migrate through the mixture.
Form meatball 1 inch for bite-size 2.5 inches for the main meatball
Can be fried or baked until browned then put into the sauce for final cooking
Let simmer in the sauce for at least two hours.

Spaghetti Sauce

1 Large onion
2 large garlic cloves
1 large roasting hen chopped into pieces
4 pork hocks
2 to 4 tablespoons olive oil
2 tablespoons oregano leaves
1-tablespoon basil
2 or 3 whole bay leaves
5 cans tomatoes 28 oz.
1 small can and 1 large can tomato paste

Put olive oil into a large stock pot
Chop onion and garlic add to stockpot simmer for about 4 or 5 minutes
Add chopped chicken, and pork hocks simmer, keep stirring do not let them stick to the bottom of the pot.
Add all spices and simmer for about 10 minutes
Add all tomatoes stir bring to boil
Add tomato paste. Stir slow boil for about 30 minutes keep stirring
Turn heat down simmer for 5 to 6 hours until desired thickness reached. If bitter at away point add small amounts of sugar teaspoon at a time until bitterness departs
Take some sauce out about 3 hours if required for meatballs. Simmer in a separate pot, for a couple of hours
Remove chicken and pork hacks at around 4-hour mark let the sauce thicken.
Serve with spaghetti or other pasta.

The Store Setup and Start-Up

Summer was just around the corner and school was just about complete. We all would be leaving Holy Cross School; I would be going into grade 9 at Hammarskjold High School. Ricky, Brucey, and Charlotte would be attending the Algonquin Street Public school just up the Street from the store. I was looking forward to the new school and starting a new chapter in life.

Our family was getting ready to make the final push, from the country farmers to city retailers. I do not remember much about moving day I can only assume, the complete move took place in one day. Family and friends were gathered to help with the work; that was just the way it was back in the day everyone came together to help. Woke up in the country and would be sleeping in the city. The furniture is gone, the room had a cold feeling void of life. I looked around my old room, sucked my pants up and walked out the door.

Next thing I knew we were heading to the new digs they were just around the corner. It did not take long to get the new place set up; it was a lot smaller than the house on the farm. The rooms, set up, furniture in place. The boy's room, down in the basement meant sharing again. Looking back, thinking I was hard done by, many people were worse off than I was; we had a roof over our heads, and all the food we could eat. Thinking back, I was a lot better at the time, than many people we knew back in the day, in fact, we were better off than many individuals today, some 50 years later. At the end of the day, the moving job complete mom served an Italian feast. Drinks, usually spaghetti and sauce with chicken and meatballs such seemed to be a staple for a family get together.

After we moved in, with living quarters established it was time to turn our attention back to the store again. The cavernous space that required stock would be the focal point for the next week. Opening day was coming only a week away, and the store was just a massive area full of shelves but devoid of any life. The next day I stayed home from school with mom and dad's blessing, the first of many deliveries arrived. It was a massive truck, 18-wheeler type. The unit was loaded with staples for the store. This first load would have been about 50% of the required stock. Uncle Nick was very involved in the setup I think he held the mortgage. As the goods came in Uncle Nick directed the delivery people so they could place the appropriate cases in the proper aisle. Soup with soup, jams with jams, cleaning supplies with cleaning supplies. Mom was at the door, and as each item came in, she would check it off against the master delivery list. In a couple of hours, the truck was empty, and the aisle ways were jammed with case's of goods from soup to nuts, everything a modern day grocery store of the mid 60's would require being a start-up venture.

Everyone took a breather; I wandered around our grocery store in amongst the cases of goods that towered over me. Boxes upon boxes would have to be unloaded and put on the shelves. The task ahead of us was daunting. This load provided the main staples for the store, many other products that were still coming. We would carry fresh produce, meat, bread, pop chips and other sundries. These all came from different suppliers, had to make sure that the coolers were arriving before the goods and the coolers we had on the site had been operating. It was nice to have

Uncle Nick to help us, there was not any wasted space, and it was now time to start emptying the cases of goods. Uncle Nick taught mom and dad how to calculate prices. There were different markups on various products I learned later. They put the amount on the cases, and we started opening the cases and marked the product with a metal ink stamper, then put the goods on the shelves making sure the rows were straight, and the product front was facing the shopper. Uncle Nick and mom were adamant; there was only one way to do this job the right way. Uncle Nick showed us some tricks on how to face and stock the shelves, so they always looked full.

Throughout the week, we continued to work getting everything ready. Go to school in the day, home as quick as possible to help stock the shelves. The coolers arrived; the penny candy and cigarette area were set up well as the ice cream, meat and produce area. The refrigerators in place and stocked. Then came the bakery area with fresh bread and Persians a Thunder Bay (Port Arthur) delicacy. From Wikipedia "A **Persian** is an oval-shaped, deep fried cinnamon-bun-like sweet roll with a sweet, pink icing made of either raspberries or strawberries. It is credited to have originated at Bennett's Bakery, and remains particular to the former city of Port Arthur, Ontario, Canada". The smell of the fresh bread made our mouths water. The store after 5 days of work was ready to open. I stood in awe, and was surprised at what we had created; our masterpiece filled with vibrant color and smells the job complete. Ricky and I, for two nights handed out flyers in the neighborhood and beyond announcing our grand opening.

The week of the grand opening was fantastic customers from the neighborhood came in to see what

[150]

we were offering it was a great success from the word go. We opened the doors and clients starting coming in. Till training began on the fly baptism by fire, so they said. Mom and Uncle Nick first, she caught on right away her five and dime training was a big help. Then Uncle Nick decided it was Dad's turn to have a shot, dad did fine, but he got frustrated when if more than one or two customers were waiting, he liked to take his time. Ricky and I were bagging goods, restocking shelves, watching over Bruce and Charlotte, helping where we could. By the time the first week was over Ricky, and I could run just about everything in the store including the old national cash register. A monster of a machine that weighed about 80 pounds. This old till was your basic cash register, added the products that were input. Gave you a total and a simplified receipt at the end of the transaction, what it did not do was tell you how much change you had to give back you had to use the countback method. Assume a customer's bill was an $8.75, and they gave me a $20.00 bill. I would give back $0.25 to make $9.00, add a $1.00 to make $10.00, then a $10.00 bill to reach $20.00. Mom and dad warned us to make sure we took our time on the count back, be polite and make sure the customer products were packed correctly. Always end the conversation with a thank you, and please come back and revisit us. As the end of a busy day approached, shelves would have to be faced, the floor would have to be mopped, Rick and I would take turns one facing the shelves and watching the counter while the other would wash the floor. So I would get the mop and bucket out add copious amounts of soap and Pine-Sol, the smell mom associated with a clean store.

This was the start of an excellent time for the family, summer was spent helping in the store. Mom getting larger now, she was seven or eight months pregnant, and she was a little slower, understandable now all these years later. So we all helped where we could. It was not all work and no play, we spent time on the beach at Boulevard Lake during the summer. When we could, we would go to the theater on Friday or Saturday night sometimes a Sunday afternoon matinee. The store was a huge success, seemed we were able to afford a few extras, a bonus considering where we came from.

After the move, the cleanup, the setup, and the grand opening of the new and improved, Agostino Forest Park Grocery store became a reality. From the Rooming House on Bay Street to the Farm on John Street, now the Store on Algonquin Avenue my short 14 years saw three significant changes in my life.

Store Uncle Nick always said make sure the shelves look neat and tidy goods lined up like soldiers.

Store with a new sign announcing we had arrived spring 1966

Sargent Major working the counter at Easter 1966

High School and a New Prince

Summer of 65, passed quickly as everyone was busy in the store, learning all the in and outs of running a new business. September rolled around, and school was starting, I was going to high school while my brothers and sister, enrolled in Algonquin Avenue public school right across the street from the store.

I started grade nine in the five-year matriculation program. This program designed for students wishing to enter university after high school. I figured that is where I belonged. It was not a good fit. I hated it, my marks were not good enough to help me through the required courses. My worst subject was French. I asked dad why he did not teach us Italian, it was the classic answer of the time, we live in Canada speak English. Learning a second language would have been a bonus at the time, but it was not in the cards.

My first week in high school was a bust. It was frosh week. We were the new kids. Expectations arose; we would do ridiculous things like wearing underwear on your head or be at the disposal of some student who thought he was better than you were. This to me was an entirely stupid way to start the journey to adulthood. Who would do these ridiculous things? Just to be accepted by a group of so-called friends, not me. As soon as frosh week was over, they disowned you like an old dirty shirt. I made a commitment to myself that as I got older, I would have nothing to do with idiotic ritual. If possible, I would help student's by-pass this dumb ritual, assist them with important things like learning the routine of a new school and a new way of life. The first month, I

[154]

stayed home quite a bit, as mom was getting ready to have the baby, not moving very quickly as she was nine months pregnant. This did not help me settle in at school but made me feel invaluable at home.

Dad's birthday was coming up, mom seemed to be waiting for a special occasion, and September 23, 1965, would be a big day in the Agostino household. Dad would be turning 41. With all the perseverance life was finally moving ahead in the right direction. Gone were the smelly coveralls, the endless days of dawn until dark and beyond hard work. The store was hard work, but it just seemed to be more comfortable, than the work on the farm. On September 23, mom went into labor, and after a short time dad got a birthday present he would never forget, the rest of us would always remember this day too. The birthday present was a little boy. Did not take long to realize he was going to be a handful. This kid was like a seagull from the shores of Lake Superior; all he did was squawk, ate and crapped regularly. So now, the family had a princess and a prince both of whom were a pain in the ass, but we loved them dearly. The princess made sure that she would take care of her little brother and made a commitment to herself that she would always be there for him. This also meant that the living quarters for the boys was about to get a bit tighter, Anthony (Tony) John Agostino was about to move in. There was a bit of a reprieve though as Tony spent his first year sleeping in mom and dad's room.

After the baby was born, dad continued working on the railway and helping in the store. He got a job back with railway cleaning cars as the company was trying everything to get him back into the fold instead of on their books as an injured employee. He was receiving a permanent injury pension, around $20.00 a month. Therefore, Dad helped in the store when he could but mom became the boss. It was a busy time for her three boys going to school age 11 to 15, 1- daughter, aged 6 and a newborn to watch over.

Dad in his coveralls with his shit stickers on his feet, (rubber boots.)

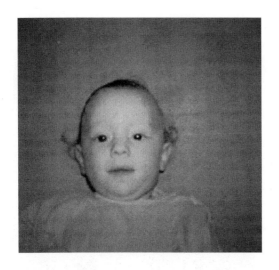

*September 23, 1965, the prince was born Anthony
John Agostino, our lives changed again. He would
say for the better. Picture Christmas 1965.*

*Christmas 1965 Aunty Teresa, Cousin Maria mom
holding the prince.*

Prince and Princess Christmas 1965, they became quite a hand full.

First Christmas in the Store

During our first Christmas in the store, Christmas of 65, mom, painstaking decorated the store and ordered a multitude of goods from Christmas candies, chocolates, cakes and other sweets as well as Japanese oranges. Growing up we usually had one or two boxes throughout the season now we could almost eat as many as we wanted. As I said, mom had the store decorated from top to bottom, and it always felt festive at this time of the year. The store is busier than normal with shoppers and the hustle and bustle of the season. People were smiling, it was an extraordinary time of the year, it was a beautiful time to be alive, and the world was full of love, peace, and goodwill. Then there were all goodies in the store, oranges, chocolates, cookies, we could have anything within reason. Life was grand.

"Tony's Joe" working counter our first Christmas in the store.

[159]

1966 a New Year

As Christmas of 65 came to a close, we were embarking on our next six months in the store. From everything, I remembered our lives were really turning around.

The rest of the school year was completed. Some of us did well and well others, let us just say these were trying times. Brucey and Charlotte did well and Rickey and I both failed. Ricky tells everyone that he liked grade eight so much that he decided to do it again. I failed grade nine. My guess the 5-year pre-university program and I were not made for each other, and my marks showed it. The worst mark was in French, 18%, that was my badge of honor I was proud of it, today I think what a waste of time I spent a whole year in school and made no advancement. So why did Ricky and I do so terrible, was it because of the move, the upheaval, the extra help we tried to provide in the store, who knows, Dad thought I was a lazy bum as far as school was concerned at least that is what he portrayed to me.

At the end of the year, the guidance counselor suggested that in fall of 66 that I should transfer to the 4-year vocational program, a program for blue-collar workers. This was a program where you had the usual core subjects, math, science, and English. With the core, subjects there would be vocational studies, woodworking, electrical, automotive all the blue-collar type jobs as well as some commercial courses typing, etc... At the end of the first two years, you would branch off into one or two specialty vocational studies for the last two years. Graduation would be next, and then get a job apprentice in your chosen field. There it was my life laid out in front of me, graduate, get an apprenticeship, get married, have kids, live in Thunder Bay for the rest of my dying days. Well, it sounded sort of good at the time, I thought to myself no this is not what I want, but I would roll with the punches for the next little while I decided what to do.

The store for the central part through this first year held its own, mom and dad felt that we were doing fine, but it took an effort from all of us to make it go. We had a Safeway store at the end of our street, which was our real competition as well as a few other corner grocery stores in the area.

The neighborhood was not flush by any stretch of the imagination. Some people lived paycheck to paycheck. Much like, we did on the farm, and we always had Uncle Nick to backstop us for groceries if the need was required. Mom and Dad had a soft heart and decided they would pay forward some of their newfound blessings. A select few needed help occasionally and mom and dad took it upon themselves to let these people charge groceries until their next paycheck. At one time, we could have up to twenty charge accounts on the go. Thinking back no one ever shortchanged us, I do remember everyone paid what he or she could.

The store was doing well, and mom's standards as high as they were, had to be followed to a tee. Ultimately, the store was clean and sharp looking. The spring of 66 was going along smoothly until I had my first encounter with death.

My First Encounter with Death

As the year went by, spring of 1966 brought me my first encounter with death. As I learned, the loss of a loved one is never trivial. I knew about the loss of life, listening to conversations mom and dad had when they lost friends, acquaintances, and distant relatives. Death was real but was never close it was always at a distance. I knew Grandpa Alfred was sick, he had been ill a very long time. Busy as we were, it just never occurred to me that death was knocking on his door. The last time I saw him was Christmas 1965. In fact, we hardly ever saw any of mom's family anymore. It was as if they vanished. To this day, I still do not know why. It just seemed to happen. The family on dad's side was very tight, and mom's side became very aloof. Then on March 21, 1966, mom got a call that Grandpa Alford had passed. He had taken a turn for the worst the week before. The store closed for a few days out of respect. This was the last time I can really remember mom's family being together as a complete unit.

1966 summer

The summer of 66 passed quickly. Our summer job was working in the store. Rick and I were competent, we could price and stock goods, do whatever was required to make the store a profitable operation. The store opened at 8:00 AM and one of us was always up and ready to go. Although this was, a busy time for us kids with lots of hard work involved we still had time for play. Instead of going to the creek for a swim, we went to Boulevard Lake, in 1901-1902 a dam was constructed on the current river, this created a man-made lake thus Boulevard Lake was born. Throughout the years, this area has been a haven for the beachgoers that lived in Thunder Bay. We spent many a summer day here; we even had money for the concession stand. The movies became the favorite pass time for the cold winter months. A favorite haunt, we could take a bus from our front door and head straight downtown to the theatres. After the movie, catch a bus back home, and we would not be too late. Some of the favorite movies at the time were the Good the Bad and the Ugly, The Sand Pebbles as well as the film, Born Free, a story about raising the orphaned lion cub. We got lost in the stories they became our adventures. The movies provided a release from the simple humdrum life we had working in the store and school. One of the sergeant majors rules. Horseplay will not be tolerated. Throughout the summer, the Sargent major was the boss of this venture.

Mom the Sargent Major

This created a different dynamic; mom was loving and caring in all the right ways, but when she donned on her white apron in the morning she might as well put on her sergeant major stripes because that's who she became.

When donned that apron she was the boss Sargent Major she came to be.

She ran the home operation with respect, control and of course, a love that was consistent with discipline and praise. There were many a time when we got into trouble, and stern warnings were handed out, we knew if we kept it up there would be severe problem's not sure what kind of trouble we would be in, but when mom spoke and was backed by dad, we knew we had better listen. Corporal Punishment could be handed out in the blink of an eye.

I remember one-day Rickey and I were fooling around in the kitchen, and we got to wrestling. There was quite a racket coming from the kitchen at the back of the store, Brucey heard mom holler you two had better quit what you are doing right now, or there will be trouble. We paid no never mind as we were having a relatively good time.

All of a sudden, Brucey was heading out the back door as quick as he could go he knew what was coming. In a matter of seconds from a warning to trouble. Mom was coming down the hall, and grabbed a brand new skipping rope and tore the packing off and made herself a good-looking strap affair. Ricky and I had shorts on as it was a beautiful spring day, and we were rolling around the kitchen floor oblivious as to what was going to happen in the next few seconds.

All of a sudden, I was sitting on top Rick; I felt a stinging sensation on the back of my legs. I realized what was happening but far too late another crack on my legs I pulled Rick over to protect me, but he realized what was going on as the skipping rope bounced off his legs he was up and scampering for the back door. This left me laying on the floor; I have never seen mom so angry, those blue eyes looked right through me, and her cheeks were puffed and red. I knew; time to get out as quick as possible. She handled that skipping rope like a boxer in training and moved it so fast that the stinging blows were intense. In a matter of seconds, I was out the door, and all I could hear was "I told you, kids, to stop, and you didn't listen," corporal punishment was intense.

Ricky and I chuckled about the going on's, and we knew we had better smarten up. Mom went back to the store; we went back to the kitchen cleaned up our mess. We went to the store a while later, told mom we were sorry, and it would not happen again, at least not at arm's length of the Sargent Major. Went about our jobs in the store all was good. Mom loved us; I think some days good old fashion discipline is what kept us all sane. We sure learned to listen, respect had to be earned not handed out like candy in the store.

1966 Fall Back To Grade 9 Again

Fall of 66 back to school, redoing grade nine only this time in the four-year vocational program. Forgot about frosh week, as I did not want to have anything to do with it. Joined the football and basketball teams this year, was a wide receiver in football until I got hurt. Was running a sideline pattern and had to turn back to catch a ball. As I turned, I grabbed the ball but my feet were planted the wrong way, and I was tackled by a huge kid, 6 foot plus probably two hundred lbs, I was around 150 lbs soaking wet, spun me around like a pretzel only thing was my foot never moved. My ankle twisted. I hobbled off the field, coach told me to suck it up, and you will be okay. In a matter of minutes, my ankle was the size of the football. Couch asked if I was ready to go back in, I said no, he never even looked at me I could tell he was pissed. After the game he said go home ice it down, we will see you at practice on Monday. Hobbled home, as soon as dad saw my ankle, of to the hospital we went, x-rays, no breaks, no tears, just a severe strain on crutches for three days. Monday went to practice coach was pissed off, not very tough are you going to let a little ankle injury hold you up. I looked him square in the eyes and said "yup." After a couple of weeks I was ready to go again but ended sitting on the bench for the remaining games, my career as a football player was over it was all right with me. I did not want to play for the jerk again. He wanted to win at all costs, forgot he was there to teach us about sportsmanship and how to have fun.

I played basketball in the winter months but was a spare as our team had many kids over six foot tall and I was a runt compared to them. Got into a few games had some fun it made that year a little more enjoyable.

The store would keep us busy after school, we took turns watching the till and working the front. We had a big enough counter so we could do homework when the store was quiet. Once eight o'clock rolled around, it was time to start the cleanup. Do the floors with pine-sol, straighten up the shelves, do the cash out lock the doors, on the way to living quarters grab a coke and a snack watch some TV and call it a night. Christmas was coming, and of course, mom had the store decked in the colors of the season. She loved to decorate it made her feel good, oh; hell it made us all feel good. It was a humdrum life tranquil. We never wanted for anything. Although we never got a wage for working in the store, we always had spending money. Mom and dad trusted us to take what we required from the till if going out for the evening to have fun. There we were settling in nicely. Our days on the farm, rapidly disappearing, we had a lot more now than ever had on the farm. We had a roof over our heads all the food we could eat, beautiful clothes, and money in our pockets, but something was missing. Not sure what I wanted to do, stay in Thunder Bay, become a shopkeeper, a tradesman or what. Something was nagging at me, there was a whole world to see, where did I fit.

Papu A Proud Man Disappears.

Once we had the store, we missed the days that Papu would come out for a visit. Papu very seldom came to the store for a visit, we had the spare lot, and he thought we should have a garden but dad told him there was no time. I remember back now and feel Papu loved the farm, as this was also part of his dream when he came to Canada to have land and grow things. We would visit him on Ontario Street; on occasion, I noticed dad and Papu sitting on his bench on the side of the house just talking the hours away. These visits were good for him, but it was just not the same as sitting by the fire cooking up a batch of slop for the pigs. When we sold the farm, I feel that his spirit just started to dwindle away. Dad got a call, on December 17, 1966. Papu had passed away. He was 84 years old and passed peacefully in his sleep. Still, to this day, I think the farm gave him life, without it, I think the will to live slowly withered away.

In less than a year, I lost both grandpas one was sick, and one just faded away. It hit the family hard no one expected this was going to happen. In one year, I learned about death twice. I was old enough to realize that death would be forever with us in our lives, as the families were getting older. No one can live forever.

The funeral was beautiful, laughter, tears hugs and well wishes were the order of the day. The oldest grandsons from each family were pallbearers, an honor bestowed upon us, and one I will never forget. The pomp and the ceremony that goes with the end of life celebration was overwhelming. The casket was massive, it took all the energy a person could muster to hold the casket level and walk in unison to the final resting spot. This was a great honor to carry this man to his last resting place. After the final goodbyes at the gravesites, the pallbearers got pats on the back for a job well done. Once we left the graveyard it was time to head to the Italian hall to complete the proceeding's, well wishes to the family were the order of the day, as well as food and coffee the men would sneak off to the member's room for something a little stronger than coffee.

I often wondered, I lost two grandparents that came to Canada from a country that they would never see again, from a country that I have never seen, their adventure now closed and mine just starting. The store closed for a few days out of respect to Papu, a great man by my recollection.

Christmas of 66 came and went although the joy of the season was subdued. The prince and princess were young, and it was a welcome relief to see the joy in these tiny faces. Another year ending.

1967-1968

The first part of 1967 went by quickly, winter, then spring and with spring came the renewal of life, as Papu would always say.

As summer of 67 rolled around Ricky and me, both succeeded in school. Ricky would be leaving Algonquin Avenue School and heading to Hammarskjold High School in the fall starting grade 9. Myself I would finally move on from grade 9 and enter 10 in the autumn. Life was very calm throughout summer, worked the store, hung out with friends, movies, and swimming. Brothers and sister were all getting older twas an annoying time.

The vocational program that I was in was okay, although none of the subjects actually jumped out at me, in fact, I could honestly say I did not like school. I was 16 now would be seventeen in the fall and was restless, not sure, what I was looking for but this lifestyle was not it. I thought maybe I should just get out of school get a job and get on with a boring life.

My limited thinking thought this was a good idea, mentioned my proposal to dad, from the reaction I got I figured I had better rethink this plan, the look that I got spoke a thousand words, none of them good. Therefore, we would try grade 10 in the fall see what it would bring. Got my driver's license dad was not a good teacher he had no patience, he had a friend who was running a driver's education school this man had an immense amount of patience and decided he would help dad out in teaching me how to drive. It went well he was an excellent instructor, and when I went for my license, first time, I passed.

[171]

Rick and I were taking music lessons. Ricky on the drums and myself it was the guitar. Rick enjoyed the drums, did really well, practicing lots. Well, practicing was not for me, and Dad knew it, I was not into it at all. Dad asked me what I wanted to do. I told him to drop guitar and take the Hunter Safety Program in the fall. I would be able to get my hunting license and then come the fall I could go hunting get back into the bush. I always enjoyed my days fishing, and the outdoors was where I belonged.

The fall of 67 came; summer was over back to school start grade 10. This was my deciding year. A decision deciding which two vocational studies would become my majors. A counselor would help me decide which subjects I might like to engage in. At the end of grade twelve I would graduate, think about working in one of my primary subjects, and get an apprenticeship work towards becoming a journeyman, so exciting, not, dad and mom were happy with this process though. By the time, Christmas rolled around my marks were satisfactory. The best two subjects were woodworking and sheet metal. Grades were in the mid-sixties I knew I was just doing enough to make it through the year. I was not happy with much of anything, did not know what I wanted or where I wanted to be. Consequently, I felt, school, was not where I wanted to be.

The second half of grade ten, I was holding my own. The subjects that I was taking were excellent, but they did not keep my interest, I was there because I had to be. As I said woodworking, sheet metal and electrical were okay fair marks, I was having a hard time with auto-shop and machine shop. Not because I could not do them, I just did not like them or the instructors.

Throughout the second half of the year, we had projects that we had to complete to get our final mark. Woodworking, make a table with dado joints, etc. job finished got a good mark. Sheet metal had to build some sort of a tin box with a multitude of different bends and folds with crazy joints. Completed, received a good mark again. Electrical had to wire a room from the plan the instructor provided and then verbally explain all the ins and outs. Job completed with average marks. That only left two more subjects and it would be off to grade eleven probably into woodworking and electrical as majors. Now the last two disciplines, automotive and machine shop, not my favorites.

A Small Problem With two Blue Collar Classes

Well in automotive we had partners, and we would work together to partially rebuild a motor. This project took more than a couple of days to do. Throughout the second half, we worked as a team and built our engine. We were marked at different stages of the rebuild, and our marks were satisfactory.

My partner was more mechanically inclined than I was, so that was a great help. We worked well, and finally, we were ready to do the final test and start our engine, we were impressed. Our instructor gave us our marks up to date we were sitting at mid-seventies, we were proud. The time came we inserted the key cranked the engine over and it roared to life. Told us to throttle up, everything looked grand, then to our dismay, there was smoke, a loud bang and quiet, our engine, just blew up. A hole on the side of the block but no oil leaking out. The instructor asked did you fill it with oil.

We looked at each other and realized that neither of us had finished this task. A simple check would have shown that we had missed the most straightforward thing in our rebuild, check the oil. In the end, we got a passing grade, just, but the instructor called me aside and recommended that I not choose automotive to be one of my primary subjects going forward.

The second incident came when I was in, machine shop. Our task was to make a ball peen hammer from scratch. First off in this class, the instructor was a stern disciplinarian, the type of person if you did not listen to him or not do things his way off to the vice principals office you would go. The vice principle always handed out some sort of discipline to the joy of this tyrant. The machines in his shop were his babies, and we were just some scum of the earth trying to disrupt his universe. As a result, this instructor was an intolerable person.

I learned in this class, slow and steady would win the race as you're dealing with steel and any amount of rushing would eventually end up with a catastrophic event. The first part of the project was to make the head. This was complete, and I got an excellent mark on it, or I thought it was excellent high 60's, but it took me longer than anticipated. The instructor told me that to get the project finished, I had better pick up the pace. Otherwise, I would not complete the task in time. This would result in an incomplete task, and it would result in a fail. I methodically started to make the handle, and this instructor never lets up, pick up the pace, get it done, time is running out. We still had a month and a half left before the end of the year so I felt I even had a lot of time left, I was not about to blow this opportunity, I needed this mark. However, there he was every class, go faster, always pushing to be faster. I ignored him and continued at my own pace the handle was coming along nicely, really taking shape and looking good if I do say so myself.

A couple of days left before the project was to be complete I was one of the last, I had two or three more trim cuts to do on the handle, and I would be complete.

On this final day, I knew I was going to finish my project. I was quietly working away, and I could see him coming over out of the corner of my eye. What was he going to say, okay job, or speed up we do not have all day? I was right the words were coming out of his mouth like a broken record, speed it up we have not got all day; I had heard these comments for the past four months. I waited until he was finished and looked at the lathe, speeded the machine up got set to take a triple cut. Engaged the bit into the medal and placed the device on automatic as he watched, it was working. Just then he noticed what I had done as I asked him if this was fast enough; he shrieked when he saw what I was doing, but it was too late the hammer handle flew out of the machine. Straight up, hit and broke a light in the ceiling came back down missed, everyone no one was hurt. The class thought it was funny, the instructor not so, so off to Vice Principal's office I went.

The VP asked me what had happened, and I explained my side of the story, I was in deep trouble, the action of the handle even surprised me I thought it would just shut the lathe down. The results were dangerous someone could have got hurt. I handed in my hammer as an incomplete project. The instructor gave me a passing grade, just, with a recommendation that I no longer consider machine shop as an option for my future. Once this was complete, I was suspended for two days because of my actions, this was bad enough, what was worse was trying to explain to dad what had happened.

Grade 10 Gone

My marks were well, good enough to get out of grade ten and into the next class.

After the episode in my machine shop class, my guidance counselor requested a meeting with me for the first morning that I got back from my suspension. He explained to me a group of educators was looking to start a new program, and they would like to interview me. I asked what this was about and the counselor explained that after meeting with my vocational instructors that they felt I really did not fit this mold and I would not succeed in any trades. I was not shocked at this because I knew my heart was not in any of the programs that I had taken for the last two years. He explained what this new program would be about, the program, called Natural Resources Technology. The new agenda would start in the fall and would have only 10 to 15 students from schools around Port Arthur. I found out later that we were kids who did not fit any of the classic molds. As a group, we were looking for something different. The new course would teach the fundamentals of prospecting, mining, and milling, forestry along with surveying. This course would give us the required basics to get a job in the resource industry when we graduated. I explained to my counselor that I was interested and would love an interview. I was accepted into the NRT program after a successful meeting with this group of educators. I was happy, but I also knew this was my last chance to get some kind of education.

I explained to mom and dad what was happening, mom was okay with it, dad, on the other hand, figured I would never amount to anything, that this was just an easy way out. I would never find a job and would become a bum. I explained to him that the resource industry was huge and there were lots of jobs, not everyone can be a tradesman. There grade 10 completed going into grade 11, the start of my new adventure.

1968 – 1969 Start the New Adventure

The summer of 68 was rather dull, we worked at the store hung out with our friends, nothing exciting happened same old same old. The war in Vietnam was going full bore. I thought to myself on more than one occasion, there had to be an adventure out there, helping all the people from the tyranny of communism. I was bored, not 18 yet but that was coming in the fall, I could make my own decisions, still wet behind the ears. Nothing could happen to me, as I was invincible. The summer passed slowly, I thought more and more about what I wanted to do, and the store did not fit into the equation, not at all, but I knew that I needed some sort of an education.

The school year would be starting in the fall of 68 in a few days. It was time to settle into the humdrum school and store routine. I was hoping that with the new program, things at school might be just a little more exciting. The new curriculum Natural Resources Technology (NRT) offered core courses, Math, English, and Science as well as other classes that would further enhance our education in the resource industry. Many of the resource courses would involve projects that required field work as well work in the classroom. The regular system of teaching would not work; we needed the outdoors to hone our skills. As a result, we would have our core courses English, Math, and Science for a minimum of two hours per day with remaining hours spent on theory for our NRT programs. This might continue for a month then we might be on the field for a couple of weeks doing practical work assignments. This system made sure that we would receive the required hours of core education and allowed us to have banked time to go into the field for two to three weeks at a time learning, surveying, geology, prospecting and mining, and forestry. We also spent time learning the required skills of snowshoeing, canoeing, power saw skills along with ax skills. These were necessary we could have a solid understanding of how to move and survive in the outdoors while doing our work. It really was going to be exciting; I met a fellow Ken Keller he was having the same problem as myself where did we fit in under the old system, so he joined the small NRT group, and we became friends for many years. Raymond's Joe and I would still see each other after school and on weekends, but our childhood bond was slowly drifting apart.

Ricky was pounding on the drums he was getting quite good at it. He would practice for hours. Would go down into the boy's room, where his drums were set up, one of his favorite drum solos, was in the song, In-A-Gadda-Divada by Iron Butterfly. When he first started working on the drum solo, it did not sound like much, but practice really did make perfect after a period of time he was, outstanding.

All four boys were in a room in the basement now. The young prince who would not go to bed by himself though. His excuse at the time, there were spiders and other creepy crawlers that lived in the basement. If the brothers were not down there to protect him, they would come and carry him off to parts unknown. We did not help matter's either because whenever we got a chance, we would tease the daylights out of him just for the fun of it. Got into trouble but it was only fun. I mean he was the birthday child. First, there was the sister then the birthday kid, so in the pecking order would be princess and prince just depending on the given day then there was the rest of the brothers. It was not all bad though they were our prince and princess and we protected them always.

Well, the young prince would go to bed, always starting out in mom and dad's room. When Rick or I went to bed, we would gather him up and take him down to his bed in the boy's room. This nightly ritual went on for some years. He would wake on occasion but would see us, and he would go back to sleep. His protectors were there. The boy's room was crowded, but it was home we were one big happy family, but on occasion, I would think there has to be more in this world than this. However, for the time beginning a roof over my head, food and family were all in ample supply. Life was good. I knew adventures were going to call my name.

A Crazy Thought

I had made up my mind that after grade eleven I was going to enlist in the American army and go to Vietnam. I could enlist, it would be a career, and I would start my adventures. The news kept showing that these poor people needed help; I was naive enough not to think that this was a power play, played by government leaders using a younger generation as pawns in a useless scheme. Maintain control of countries under the guise of protecting democratic rights of a foreign country. I figured that I would wait until I graduated from grade eleven before I sprung this idea on mom and dad.

Well taking core subjects in overdose amounts one of the things I remembered was an English teacher teaching us about poetry. I enjoyed this class and at night well sitting in the store, I would write poems about the war in Vietnam, before long I had a book of probably twenty to thirty poems. I gave them to my English teacher at the end of the year for her scrutiny and never saw them again. Do not know whatever happened to them. Going through a box of old keepsakes, I came across one of my originals that never made it into the book. A Calling Unheard was one of the earlier poems that I wrote. I was starting to have second thoughts about this adventure.

A Calling Unheard

Across the ocean,
In a place called Vietnam.
A place that I had not seen,
A jungle that was lush and green.

Bombs were dropping.
Bullets were flying.
People were dying.
They just wanted to be free.

I sat alone one night,
The store empty and cold.
Radio in the background playing,
Peter, Paul, and Mary Leaving on a jet plane.

It came to me that night,
Soon I would be 18.
Vietnamese people needed my help,
What an adventure this would be.

Bullets could not harm me,
I was invincible you see.
I would join,
To help these people be free.

The reality of war,
I had not seen.
Soon I thought,
I would be in a jungle lush and green.

The news, that night,
Showed people crying in despair.
The jungle colored red,
Was not lush and green.

I would have to rethink,
This adventure to be.
As the invincible people before me,
We're left, lying on the jungle floor.

Bullets tore them apart,
Dying in a land far away,
As they took their last breath,
The thought of helping these people slowly faded
away.

The start of the school year in 68 I had my life mapped out quit school and join the US army. I would be 18 in a month. I figured let us get this adventure on the go. Finish grade 11, sneak down to Duluth, Minnesota, join the US army and go to Vietnam, I was gonna go on a real adventure. It was a good plan I thought, I never did talk to dad about it, and I knew his answer would be resounding no. I kept the idea to myself I do not understand why I was waiting until the end of grade 11 to pull this off, must have, had an angel watching over me maybe Papu was watching me from the heavens.

Who Was That Person

The year was going according to my plan, school was going excellent, I was enjoying it, and my marks were better than they had been all my life. Not banner mind you but at least acceptable. Then Christmas of 68 came lots of snow and lots people in and out of the store. The store was dressed to the nines the way mom liked it. On Saturday between Christmas and New Year's, I was working in the store one particular afternoon. It was a snowy day, I was looking out into the schoolyard across the street, and I could see two people trudging through the snow. Little did I realize my life was about to change forever.

I thought they must be from the Oak Avenue area on the other side of the schoolyard coming to catch the bus just outside the store. I watched for a while then continued to stock the penny candy shelves and the cigarette shelves. At this time, the candy was lower shelves and cigarettes were above. Candy was usually three for a penny, cigarettes were thirty-five cents for a pack, and you could buy a package of smokes if you were 16 or you had a note from your parents.

I looked out again, and they were crossing the street coming into the store. I could not figure out why they did not go to Safeway's just up the road must have been fate all the better for us. They finally made their way to the store, and I said hello. They were new in the neighborhood. After two and half years of running the store, we knew most people in the area, and the new ones always stuck out just by their demeanor. They asked a few questions as they shopped around and found everything they were looking for. They used one our grocery carts and brought everything up to the till. I totaled the goods and proceeded to put them in Brown paper bags. I realized they would have a hard time carrying these products home. I decided to place the groceries in brown bags then shopping bags; it would make it easier to cart. As I was doing my thing, I struck up a conversation with them. The mom who was a small thing told me they had just moved from Saskatoon and were living on Oak Avenue.

My first Picture of Carol

I looked at her daughter guessed she was around 16, long brown hair and greenish brown eyes, the prettiest thing I had ever seen. I thought that I had ice water in my veins but seeing her, she melted my disposition, and I would have been putty in her hands at that moment. Before I knew it, they were going out the door, and I never got her name. Thinking that is someone I would like to get to know, hopefully, I would see her before school started in a week.

A couple of days later she entered the store again along with her sister. They went about their business and finally came to the counter to pay for their goods.

Introduced myself as I was totaling their purchases. Proceeded to ask, "What's your name," a little giggle, she was not going to say anything, and her sister spoke out "my name is Heather and this my older sister Carol." I looked at her square in the eyes, well I was like a lovesick calf, she was the sweetest person I have ever met, and good looking. Found out she was going to Hammarskjold High in grade thirteen, the five-year program for those wishing to go to university. Thought to myself, will never have a chance with her once she meets all the goody two shoe students. Doctors and lawyers and such vs. the shopkeeper, NRT student not much of a chance at any kind of relationship there. Was she going to be a snob just like the rest of them?

Well over the next couple of weeks, she came to the store a few times. We had a few more conversations; with each visit, I had the opportunity to get to know her a little better. I was a lot more relaxed around her now as compared to the first day I saw her. She did not just get her goods she would stay for a bit before she left. The prince and princess started bugging me. Joey has a girlfriend. Told them to be quiet or I would feed them both to the creatures that lived in the basement. That kept them silent for a while.

Back to school now hoping that one day I would bump into Carol. One day I was talking to Raymond's Joe up in the commercial wing of the school. Bumped

[188]

into Carol on my way out. Asked her if she wanted company on her way home, she said sure. I grabbed her books and walked her home. Now I knew her name and where she lived, was not sure what the future would hold, would just have to wait and see.

Outers Club

As school started in 68, one of the extracurricular activities we had to belong to was the outers club. This organization enhanced our NRT studies, giving us experience in the movement of goods in summer and winter without the use of motorized equipment such as canoes and snowshoeing.

The fall of the year, we would portage our canoes from the school to the waterfront a distance of three to five kilometers depending where we launched. Once the canoes were placed into the harbor, we would canoe around the Lakers and the Salties. As long as they were anchored, it was safe. We would do this a couple of times a week until the foul fall weather moved in; canoe for a couple of hours then portage back to the school. This was great exercise and an excellent way to build stamina and create teamwork amongst ourselves as well as getting our completive juices flowing, see who could portage the fastest, etc. this extra work got us in shape for what was coming in the winter months. This was a great club to belong to, and it did help with our NRT studies. The membership into this association was not limited to anyone, but it seemed that the majority of the participants were from the five-year program. That created a little dislike but also created a real competitive atmosphere, as these students were not going to outdo us. During the fall, our cores consisted of canoeing, surveying, wildlife studies, and other activities that were required to fulfill our NRT course load. The ministry of Natural resources required some help in collecting biological samples, hunting demographics and other information from the fall moose hunt. The preservation of the animal required this information to facilitate the longevity of the hunt in this part of northwestern Ontario. After the hunting season closed, it was time for core subjects then Christmas and a couple of weeks away from school.

Carol and I knew each other, so to speak, if we saw each other at school we would say hi. She became friendly with a group in grade thirteen. These students I knew a few of them reasonably well as they were in outers along with NRT class. Some were friendly, others were snobs and would not have anything to do with us lowly NRT boys, we were in grade eleven, although we were older than the majority, we just had more life experiences than they did. I think to this day, some of these kids were just jealous. They had the books and the classroom; we had books, the classroom and the great outdoors. Carol joined outers at the end of January. The NRT boys were already going out for overnight snowshoe hikes, building lean-tos, learning how to set up winter camp, staying dry and learning how to exist on hydrated rations. Come February everyone in outers was going out for snowshoe hikes after school a couple of times a week. This was building up stamina for longer hikes that would take place at the end of February and throughout March. It was our job to train and get these kids in shape for the longer walks. Some of the snobs really did not like the fact that we lowly NRT people were doing the training. To us, it did not matter just do what you are supposed to do and quit your bitching. Carol was a joy to be around she was like a sponge gathering all the information that we could provide. I was there any time she needed something, my motive, well known by my fellow classmates, I was going after this girl, and I was going to catch her. Carol and I became friends, and then we became an item, my first girlfriend. Getting to know her put a stop to my thinking about going to the U.S. and joining the army at the end of the year. The war in Vietnam will have to be someone else's adventure as my adventure turned 180 degrees after I met Carol.

Snowshoe Hike

Through the winter months, the NRT group would go snowshoeing and on overnight hikes. One time in mid-march there was a 15 to 20-kilometer trek that the outers group was going on. They would leave the school around 4 pm and would arrive back around 11 pm that same night.

The club took a bus out to the country, from the drop-off point they would snowshoe back to the school, on a predetermined course. This trip required two volunteers from the NRT group to go out and break trail on this route so the group following would be able to keep up a solid pace. My buddy Ken and I volunteered for this task, we left school at 1 pm got a ride out to the predestined start point and were dropped off with our gear and compasses and a map showing the course. We each carried a pack with some dry clothes a light lunch, as we would be out on the trail throughout the evening. We learned later that this was part of our testing, for our final mark on winter preparedness. Therefore, off we went chattering as if we were a couple of squirrel's discussing everything from girls to life-altering decisions we would have to make in the future. It got dark early, not a problem, we followed our map and used our compasses to keep on track. After about an hour, we hit the creek. The creek was the final leg of the journey travel for about 5 kilometers on the creek then get off, we would have about a kilometer left to get to the school. We had been traveling on the creek, went about a kilometer, and we decided we should get off make a fire and have some lunch. We kept hearing some noise as we walked but decided it was just the ice and snow settling under our weight. There was no slush where we were walking, so we assumed we were on some solid footing. We stopped and were talking, about lunch; we heard some strange cracking noises then a loud swooshing sound. We figured we had better get off the river as something was happening, as we started heading to the shore I could see the water beginning to rise on Ken's snowshoes, as he was I front of me, I yelled at Ken get moving. The ice just sank from under us were going to be swimming in a matter of seconds. We scampered up the shore, wet up to our knees, we looked at the river it was an incredible sight. The moon reflected off the water which just a few minutes ago was snow and ice.

Got our bearings, built a fire, had a bite to eat, changed our socks dried off a bit and contemplated our next move. We knew that the remaining trip was going to be rougher as we would have to traverse the shoreline of the river, develop a trail as we went. The group was about four hours behind us. We figured we could break a new path then head back to the team before they got into the creek area and got into trouble.

Ken and I headed back upriver to the point where we moved onto the creek. The ice had dropped to this point we could see water flowing over the top of the ice. We started marking out the trail in this location using fluorescent flagging tape. Followed the creek and marked the path as we went. We picked out the more accessible areas to walk. After a couple of hours, we left the creek area, the remaining trail was straightforward, one could follow the roads or walk the ditch line. We were only a mile or so from the end of our journey. We dropped our packs hid them in the underbrush and headed back to the main group.

We caught the leading group about a half-mile from the river explained the changes in the route, we got thanks for letting them know and joined up with the group. I found Carol and slipped in behind her, and we talked all the way back. Once we arrived at the river Ken, and I took, turns leading the group as we knew where we were going. Around eleven pm we entered the school. There was a dance going on, some of the participants who were on the walk went to the dance, and some stayed back for some hot chocolate and conversation. It was a grand night; we were tired but had a real sense of accomplishment. Walked Carol home she wanted to know what I was doing on Saturday night told her I had to work in the store; she was more than welcome to come and keep me company. She decided she would we said good night and I kissed her, my first real kiss. Neither of knew how long this was going to last but what the heck, let's go for the ride and see what happens. It was a night to remember. My marks were better, I was enjoying school, life was grand, and Carol kept me grounded.

One of the many snowshoe hikes we took while in NRT.

The Beast

Dad bought Ricky and me a car in the early spring of 69, which we shared. It was not much of one, an old 1951 green Pontiac flathead six, a tank, made of pure steel was extremely heavy. It was ours, and gave us freedom; the only thing was that if you ever went up long hills, you were taking your life into your own hands. Usually, as you reached the crest it would, cough and sputter, sometimes it would quit, but 90% of the time, it made it. Other times we would pull over give the beast a rest then in about 15 minutes get going again.

The reason this beast came about was that one Saturday in early spring dad let me take his car out to Shebandowan Lake. A big black Chrysler station wagon could carry many people. We were going out to the lake to shovel a friend's summer camp roof off, enjoy the day a little work and lots of fun. I drove to school and picked Carol up on the way then stopped and picked up the rest of the crew. There were two cars, and we wanted to see who would get there first. We left and headed out highway 102 towards Kaministiquia, the roadway was clear, and it was a beautiful drive. Decided to speed up a bit so we could catch up with the other car. Driving along we were coming up to the Kaministiquia river going down a steep hill the car speeded up, as we hit the bridge there was black ice, and we spun out going sideways down the road with the front end riding on the snow bank on the right-hand side of the road. We came to a stop everyone was okay, a bit shaken up. Got out had a look at the front end everything seemed fine?

Continued our journey, the car handled fine, arrived at our destination and proceeded to have a great day.

Drove back home, dropped everyone off and thanked dad for the use of his car. Never said a thing about what had happened. A few days later dad was out driving, and the car was acting funny, brakes very spongy. Dad decided to take it in, well the mechanic asked dad, what had he hit, dad said nothing. The mechanic said somebody hit something. The mechanic found some damage, bent brake lines that were leaking. This the most serious problem. Repairing these lines will get you back on the road.

Dad got home and called me into the kitchen, "do you want to tell me what happened to my car" busted, proceeded to tell him what happened he was furious with me. What made him the maddest was that I tried to cover it up. From that time we could only use his car on special occasions, it had to be unique or no dice. So then, to solve dad's problem of us keeping our hands off his car he purchased the green beast. Thinking about that day, I must have had a guardian angel riding with me. It could have been catastrophic.

Dads New Yorker his pride and joy.

Canoe trip of 1969

Spring rolled around, marks were all right, and I was really enjoying the outdoors. My scores were excellent in my NRT subjects marginal in my core subjects. It was time to get in shape for the annual end of year canoe trip for the outers. The NRT students were going on this voyage, as it was part of our curriculum. Once the ice on Lake Superior left the harbor, we started our bi-weekly routine of portaging our canoes from the school to the waterfront, launch, and then canoe in the harbor around the Lakers and the Salties, which were anchored in the bay. Then pull out and cart our equipment back to school.

Before the year was finished, we had one more excursion to complete. This outing would be a co-ed joint venture including outers and NRT students. For the NRT students, this was another training exercise to complete our yearly studies. The trip itself would be an excruciating fourteen-day venture that would cover 220 to 260 kilometers, numerous portages, rain or shine. We would have to average 20 kilometers a day this would give us two days throughout the journey to rest and catch our wind.

Each canoe had a crew of three people, ours, two other fellows from class and me. Our gear was made up of hydrated rations, 3 man tents, sleeping bags, cooking equipment, personal gear, axes, compasses, etc. each back weighed around 70 lbs. The canoe empty was between 80 to 110 pounds.

Day one we arrived at our launch point, French Lake in Quetico Provincial Park. The park is a vast wilderness park located in northwestern Ontario well known for its excellent canoeing and fishing. Located just south of Atikokan, a small town known for a couple of massive iron ore mines, Steep Rock and Caland Iron Ore. The two operations started here in the mid-fifties. To start mines, built dams, drained lakes, and rerouted rivers. Once completed the mines became operational. The first iron ore, shipped by rail from this area in 1960. Its destination, the newly constructed iron ore dock in Port Arthur (Thunder Bay North). Both mines closed down in the 1979/1980.

We arrived mid-morning and proceeded to offload the gear from the bus. The canoes were loaded, and we were ready to cast-off around noon. I thought we were in good shape with all of our practicings after school. Found out that the only thing we actually learned on our after-school trips were the mechanics of rowing. After about four hours of paddling, our canoe was in the last place, and I thought to myself we had better pull up our socks, or this is going to be a long trip. Paddled about 10 kilometers the first day. Realized the next few days we would have to do more than 20 kilometers per day to maintain the average. Everyone was docking we were about 15 minutes behind. Landed found a place to set up camp took us about a half hour, and then it was time for something to eat we took out a packet of rations got some water started a fire and cooked the hell out of our dry food. After about a half hour of boiling this stuff we ate. It was eatable, no spices, and no taste. After our meal, we sat around and discussed our plan on how we could get better at what we were doing. We knew we needed a plan; our first day was a bust. It would take a couple of days to get our arms, legs, and backs in shape. We could not let those five-year kids beat us at our own game. Bunch of smart-ass kids, they were out doing us. All year we had gone on trips with the NRT group they were not long, but the key to success

[199]

on any of these trips was the detail we spent on planning, planning to the smallest detail. With this in mind, we decided as a group to come up with a plan to make this trip better, without it, it was going to be a long fourteen days.

Our plan dictated that we would have to decide on meals ahead of time so we could prepare this grub to make it eatable. One thing Papu had taught me about dried foods is that they always taste better if they are soaked ahead of time give the spices a chance to blend. So in the morning, we decided we would take one of our big pots fill it Spanish rice or dried stew or soup whatever we decided we would have and let it soak for the day. The container would sit in the bottom of the canoe, braced in an upright position, kept the food in the pot. As a result, after a full day of soaking, we just would heat it up, and it would be ready for our evening meal. We looked at our gear and decided to be a team we would have to be organized. Therefore, we reorganized our equipment. All the food and cooking stuff went into one pile, sleeping gear into another heap the third collection of material was our personal gear. From here our three backpacks were loaded. Now our equipment was sorted made for easier setups when we landed for meals or camp for the night. When I cleaned out my pack, I had some foodstuffs, spices, salt and pepper, and three pounds of coffee and sugar. Our foodstuffs just got better, and well my partners just smiled. Simple things just made our day.

The next morning after breakfast, pancakes, the canoes were loaded, and we set off. Felt a lot better we were somewhat organized. Knew it was going to be a long day. The sun was out, and there was a slight breeze, which kept us cool. The lakes were clear and cold. When thirsty just dip your cup into the lake and have a drink. Best water I have ever tasted. After about five hours of paddling, we hit our first portage, this was a real gong show, total disarray, not much teamwork, and no organization after an hour we all made it through it should have only been a fifteen to thirty-minute walk. Once we were finished with the portage, we made lunch. Built a small fire and heated up what was going to be our supper and in no time we were eating. We then realized we would always have to have a pot of rations soaking. We could stop and have a bite to eat anytime. Salt and pepper made the dish a lot more bearable. Back into the canoe and away we went. My muscles burned and were sore, arms, my back, and legs cramped up, my hands were sore from banging on the side of the canoe. Thought to myself and wondered, this has to get better, get back in shape, suck it up and quit whining. I was not going to give up. We made the twenty-five kilometers that day, but our team dead tired when we hit the shore. Set up camp and had supper. This time after dinner, we made ourselves a cup of coffee. The smell of coffee wafted through the air. Was not long we had company; people were stopping in for a visit with their coffee cups. We knew we would have to ration the coffee if we wanted it to last for the fourteen days. We were hospitable though and gave away what we could. That cup of coffee still lingers in my taste buds to this day. We decided to have a chat and plan our next day, it was going to be another long day twenty-five kilometers or more with two or three portages. We discussed as a group how we would handle the portages. Each one of us had a job to do as soon as we docked. We knew what we had to do. The meal menu for the next day, was established, made some dehydrated biscuits for lunch and prepared what we could for breakfast, lunch would be soup and biscuits the evening meal was going to be dehydrated stew. Thank the lord for salt and pepper. Put our gear away, and hit the sack, had a great sleep.

Morning came, up and ready to go. Coffee and pancakes, lunch soaking in the pot packed up canoe loaded sitting in the bay waiting for the gang. First time for us to be on the water before anyone else, it was not the last. The planning was paying off. After about an hour, the muscles loosened up we were in the middle of the pack. Hit the first portage after a couple of hours of paddling. It should only take an hour to complete the crossing. Our planning went into gear. The first person out of the canoe grabbed a pack, our pot of soaking food in one hand and an ax in the other and started making off down the trail. My partner and I finished unloading the canoe through a pack on our backs, picked up the canoe and started heading down the path. We met our partner on the trail he was heading back, gathered up our loose odds and sods and made it back to the other side of the portage just as we were finishing putting the gear back into the canoe. Got everything in the canoe and pushed off done in forty-five minutes, sitting in the bay having a drink of water waiting on the other canoes.

Saw Carol almost every day but no alone time with her. As we sat waiting, we analyzed the portage that we just completed, and decided we could do better, make it all in one trip. Within the hour, everyone was done and back on the water, we were not first, but not last, decided, between the three of us we wanted to be first all the time. Paddled for a couple of hours and then stopped for lunch, soup and biscuits were grand. Took off after our meal hit the second portage within an hour, our plan worked, loaded everything we could. Took it all in one hit. We made it to the end of the portage, dropped the gear.

[202]

Made it record time, loaded our gear into the canoe, we were ready to go, and we decided we would go back and help some of the other crews, teamwork. We were feeling good about ourselves when we pushed off, one more portage for the day we paddled until late made our twenty-five kilometers, landed made camp. Well, we were paddling after the last portage we put out a fishing line and let it ride behind the boat within a few minutes we had caught a couple of northern pikes, fish for supper and breakfast. Living the good life. After our meal coffee again by the campfire, few more visitors, down to the lake to wash up dishes met Carol stole a good night kiss. What an adventure.

Canoe trip with outer's spring 1969

The remaining days were excellent, paddling, portaging, fishing, healthy meals and stealing the occasional kiss. We covered a lot of ground, and on the last day, we stopped short left us about 7 kilometers to do the next day. We could go for a swim, try to get cleaned up, have one more real feast of fish and Spanish rice, couple pots of coffee. Lots of company the outer's kids were not that bad, we bonded with a lot of them, and they became good friends. The year was ending, finish the trip in the

[203]

morning pack up, and ride the bus back to Thunder Bay then go our separate ways. More than one relationship had been established over the previous 14 days. The last night was going to be grand; plans were made to make it a memorable last night once our chaperones were sleeping. Well, they were not as dumb as we thought they were, just as we were done with the swimming washing up clothes cleaned, the girls were told pack up get back into their canoes head out to the island about 1000 meters of shore. That brought the evening to an end. Hormones were put to bed to come alive another day.

The next morning, we packed up, at a leisurely pace, left and headed for the launch point. Twas a beautiful paddle, lots jabbering back and forth. Once we landed everyone pitched in. Helped unload the canoes, load the bus for the trip back to Thunder Bay, it was a quiet journey.

Grade eleven was now finished, I would be moving on to grade twelve, and Carol would be going to Confederation College. Would our love last. High school was over for a large group of these kids. They would start a new journey. I had one more year in high school. The past year was a great year. I could only hope that my last year in high school would be as grand. A year from now I would graduate and start a new journey.

Summer 69 Welcome to CNR

There was three of us to help in the store in the summer of 69 myself, Ricky and Bruce, Charlotte was starting to do some things, and the prince well lets us just say he was there, pain in the ass, but loved him just the same. I figured should be an easy summer lots of free time. Dad had a different idea, he felt it was time for me to get out and get a summer job. The store was in capable hands with Ricky and Bruce as well as mom overseeing the operation, and it was time to start earning my own keep.

Twas around the middle of July dad pulled some strings and got me a summer job working on the railway, on the repair track over in Westfort. No store for me this summer a real job, would like to show him just how good a worker I could be.

Dad was working here too, so I got a ride to work with him the first morning. As I entered the staging area first thing, I noticed was a multitude of languages being spoken, very little English. Dad introduced me to the supervisor. Now this fellow was not friendly, no hello, good morning or go to hell nothing at all. He looked at me and finally said fresh meat, will see how long you will last. Thought to myself I was gonna last six weeks, then back to school and no red necked supervisor was going to run me off. I would do what was required each day. It started my working career, working for the man. Each day I was assigned a multitude of tasks worthwhile or not. I was a runner for the Carmen. Would be consistently getting them supplies. It was hot on the repair track, dark ground and surrounded by boxcars, blocking any breeze if there was any. One of the first jobs that I had to do each day was to make sure that cold water was placed in the coolers along the track. The men working here required ample water to keep hydrated throughout the day.

The repair track was long, had three tracks with a 20-foot buffer between the sets of rails. This barrier made up of gravel in the middle and sandy material by the tracks. This sandy material alongside the tracks stuff had become laced with used oil and grease; the working conditions were quite dirty. My duties for the summer consisted of a variety of jobs throughout each day, once my regular tasks were complete, the supervisor explained to me that he wanted these work areas along the tracks cleaned up. Remove the dirty sands and replace with clean sand. I got my tools for my summer work, a wheelbarrow, and shovel. After my second week I started doing this job, a daunting task, it was going to be complete before I left and returned to school, that was my goal. It started with wheelbarrow after wheelbarrow of dirty sand, replaced with clean sand. After the first couple of days of doing this, I was always trying to figure out a way that I could stay and do other jobs on the repair track but to no avail. This job was the shits; this went on for four weeks. I finally got it complete with about a week to spare. The supervisor saw that I had completed this enormous task, he said now go down the tracks and clean any areas that look dirty again. This was a never-ending job. I looked at him and as if he had rocks in his head, thought to myself, you are just a miserable power hungry man, as I went on my way to carry on with my wheelbarrow and shovel.

Before my final week, I thought maybe this would be a good job, learn how to use the tools and become a Carman on the railway forget school and get on the railway. Therefore, I talked to my supervisor one day, decided to ask him about the future. I told him I might like to stay on if possible get a full-time job, how long would it take to get on the tools and do something different more in line what the other workers were doing. How long would I have to labor before I could get on the tools? After a long pause, he looked me in the eyes and asked what do you have for an education. I told him that I had grade eleven. Again a pause and then he said, well kid after six weeks I was still a kid, would not even call me by my name. Then he proceeded, and he told me well kid probably next five years you got the tools you'd be using the wheelbarrow and a shovel. No education, no brains, just do the job you were hired to do. I will do the thinking, you do the shoveling you dumb ass dago. This guy was Italian and a supposed friend of dads. I remembered when I was called that name way back in my school days, I was furious, this guy was big, and he was my boss, so I just took it, finished my shift and went home. That night while working in the store, I realized my railway career was ending. Only a few days left and then back to school. The next morning I went back, started my tasks, and knew I would have everything complete by Friday's end. Friday came, and I said goodbye to everyone, my job complete. The supervisor said Joe you did a good job, if you are looking for work next year, look us up. I am sure the wheelbarrow, the shovel will be waiting, and a strange smirk came over his face as I said my goodbyes. I thought to myself, my railway career is over and thank God for that. I can honestly say that I never looked back, never tried to get a job on the railway again. I walked out of the yard and thought to myself, grade twelve will be a piece of cake after this summer job.

Years later, when I was chatting with dad, we talked about that summer on the railway. He told me he orchestrated the job on the railway to be the worst

[207]

summer job a kid could have, dad, did not want me working on the railway. The supervisor and dad decided that I would get the worst jobs possible. Dad was proud even though at the time he could not say it. I stayed did the shit jobs never quit; learned perseverance and patience are good traits to have.

Although the summer of 69 I spent working on a real job, never considered working in the store for mom and dad a job, it was just what you did growing up when your parents had a small business.

Summer 69 Playtime

Carol got a job working on the railway with her father in the express sheds, secretarial help. Her dad was somewhat of a tyrant and a controlling SOB, and he did not like me one bit. Carols dad came into the store one day and proceeded to tell me to stay clear of his daughter. He felt I would not amount to much. Mom overheard him I let him have it with both barrels. Carol and I did a lot of sneaking around that summer.

When Carol's family went on vacation, we spent an enormous amount of time together, and it proceeded to be a summer of firsts for both of us. We were in love, although we were not sure what love was, we enjoyed being with each other. Life was grand. So after that two weeks, we never cared what her dad thought, we just carried on with life, he would have to accept what we had, at least that is what we hoped. Mom and Dad were happy with our relationship. Dad took a real shine to Carol he really liked her. Told me, not to burn the candle at both ends, his comments when I was getting ready for work one morning. All he said was "did you sleep last night?" I said "yes," and he looked me square in the eye and said, "not here, be careful and do not tell your mother what you're up to." Carol's mom was a sweetheart; I got along with her incredibly well although she thought the relationship was a good fit but just moving a bit too quickly.

With our new car, the 51-Pontiac beast Carol and I would go on adventures all summer. One of the favorite haunts was up to the Spruce River Road, we would go for picnics, fishing or just lazing around and enjoying each other's company.

Carol's dad continued to make life miserable for us. Some nights she would end up staying home, or if we went out there was usually an unreasonable curfew be home by 10, or you will be grounded. I would make sure she was back on time. We were just biding our time until he was out of the picture. When Carol couldn't get away, or I brought her home early, sometimes I would just go out cruising with Ken or Raymond's Joe. It was a busy summer lots of fun, lots of love, lots of work, many adventures and no thoughts of escaping and going off and looking for new experiences. Then, summer was over, sure seemed short not like when I was a kid on the farm, summer lasted forever. I was going back to Hammarskjold and Carol was off to Confederation College. Would our love hold?

Final Year in High School September 1969

September of 69 came, and I realized this was it, finish this year and embark on life. Where should I go, would I be single, where would the road of life take me, would Carol and I stay in love, will our love grow or will it die like so many other high school relationships.

I was about to be 19 in a month, Ricky 17, Bruce 15, Charlotte 10, and the little prince Tony would be 4. Come a long way from the block on Bay Street and the small farm on John Street. Time was marching on.

Grade 12 started with a new look, Jim Smithers no longer teaching NRT but still leading the outers club. A new fellow Danny Langille a mining professional, someone who understood the industry, mining, forestry, and other resource industries in the area. His knowledge would change the scope of my last year in high school from one of the academics mixed with a small smattering of resource technology to one of the academics with a large smattering of natural resource technology. There would be a massive amount of hands-on education as well a robust main course curriculum. Dan explained to us that we could be in our core courses for two, three or up to six weeks at a time.

The two main things I remember about this last year was, we took a school trip where we traveled through parts of Ontario, Minnesota, Wisconsin, and Michigan. A journey where we would travel over 3200 kilometers (2000 miles). A mining company hired the NRT group if I remember correctly. We were to do some line cutting and claim staking, in the

Pardee / Devon township area south of Thunder Bay. The task started in February and went for six to eight weeks. The remaining time, spent in the classroom and on core subjects and short journeys around Thunder Bay getting a solid understanding of the resource opportunities in our area. Graduation culminated the year, closed the door on being a kid, and started the journey into manhood.

The Trip

This was an exciting time for me. My travels in life consisted of a trip to Winnipeg, to visit some relates while I had some dental work done. Why Winnipeg for dental I am not sure, I think it was cheaper at the time. The only other place that I had gone was to Schreiber to visit relatives. So this trip for me was a real first, I was starting to spread my wings a real journey.

We had an older school bus that we used for traveling in. Took out the back seats so we could store our gear and coolers. The journey was a minimal cost trip so all NRT grade 12 students could participate. We would be staying in school gyms and YMCAs when possible. Eat out nothing fancy and have stuff in our coolers for lunches etc. The journey would be a round trip with overnight stops in Duluth, Ishpeming, Green Bay, Milwaukee, Chicago, Detroit area, Mackinaw City, Sault Saint Marie, and Wawa and back to Thunder Bay.

This would be an educational trip where we would be touring natural resource operations from fish and wildlife, mining operations, agriculture operations as well as plant manufacturing. We left Thunder Bay, crossed the border at Pigeon River south of Thunder Bay on Highway 61, and proceeded to Duluth, Minnesota on the way we stopped at a fish habitat venture and multiple rock outcrops studying the geolocation formations. The next day we traveled to Marquette / Ishpeming area. This area is known for its taconite operations. Taconite is low-grade iron ore. Here for a couple of nights, visited a couple of large taconite operations. I found the mining operations invigorating. I knew then this is where I wanted to head. The diesel engines roaring to life, drilling, blasting were all exciting aspects of the operation.

From here, our journey took us to Green Bay, Wisconsin, the land of cheese and the Green Bay Packers. Toured cheese plants again a good understanding of the resources to make cheese. I was more interested in the Green Bay Packers. They became my favorite team in American football. Much like my Saskatchewan Roughriders, community-owned an operated.

Off to Milwaukee, visited the Schlitz brewery. A full half-day tour. Again, a fascinating way to involve natural resources, water, and farming, but not for me. The drinking age at the time was 21, so the only thing we missed was the tasting room.

Headed to Chicago for an overnight stay. Toured around in the afternoon went out for pizza and stayed in a high school gym just a bit away from the downtown core. After we were settled in, a few of us decided we would walk downtown. We were on the major street so it would be a short hike to get down to the waterfront area. Headed out and started making our way to the waterfront, we were coming up to a five or six block area that didn't look too inviting, just older is all. One must remember we were not travelers of the world just a bunch kids from small-town Canada. We proceeded, crossed the street before we got 100 feet a police car pulled up beside us and stopped, lights going. We were dumbfounded and wondered what had we done. The officer got out, and we knew enough not to be smartass, answer all questions. The first question who are you, we explained who we were, from where we came and what we were doing. The officer told us this is not a

[214]

safe area for strangers to walk through. We said we were just going downtown, close to the lake it was only 10 blocks. Again, he explained we could not walk through this area. We asked about the bus. He said not recommended either. Told us to jump in, and he would give us a ride. We did, and away we went. Phenomenal to see Chicago. One thing I do remember is we came up to an intersection and traffic was backed up in every direction. Next thing we saw was a Red Corvette driving up with lights and sirens going. A cop car. A large man wiggled his way out of the car, went to the intersection, and started to direct traffic. I thought we had moves when we were dancing, but we could not hold a candle to this guy. Before we knew it, the gridlock was cleared, and the vehicles were moving in every direction, within 15 minutes he was gone. We made it back to our lodging for the night and the next morning headed out to the Detroit / Flint area.

We drove seemed like forever, overpasses, underpasses, and people going 1,000 miles an hour at least it looked like it, but after an hour, we were clear. I thought to myself, we will be stuck here for eternity. Map reading proved to be valuable.

We arrived in the Detroit area and set up around Flint, stayed in a YMCA. The next day toured an automotive plant and visited a museum. This was an excellent opportunity to see how the raw products, iron ore were developed into fenders, bumpers, etc., mostly everything at this time was made of metal. Once we completed our tours in this area, we knew the trip was ending. It was time to start heading home.
From here, we traveled north to Mackinaw City moved over the Mackinac Bridge a suspension bridge, 8,000 meters (8,748 yards) long. We were on the largest

[215]

structure crossing a body of water that I had ever seen. This spanned the Straits of Mackinac and joined the upper and lower peninsulas of the state of Michigan. On one side, Lake Michigan and on the other Lake Huron. A feat that took three years to build. From here, we continued north and reached Sault St. Marie.

While in the Sault, we toured the locks a system of waterways that allow ships, freighters, and salties to navigate the 21-foot drop between Lake Superior and Lake Huron. The other place of interest was the Algoma steel mills, this was a grand tour as we saw the raw iron ore molded into steel.

Once we completed the tours, we headed to Wawa Ontario. Here we toured a couple of gold operations. Went underground and got a real appreciation for how underground operations worked. One thing I do remember, it was cool, and dark and dirty. There was an actual system on how it worked from drilling, blasting, mucking then moving the blasted muck to the surface for processing. This was mining, this was where my interests laid.

Finally, the day came when we headed for home Thunder Bay. After twelve to fifteen days on the road. Once home we had to do a detailed report on everything we saw and how each aspect of the trip related to the different natural resource areas. We learned that natural resources industry is extensive and varied and did not just consist of mining and forestry.

The Camp Job

Next project consisted of a mining exploration job. The time frame for working and completing this job, February / March. This particular job was located in the Pardee / Devon Township area south of Thunder Bay. We had a claim map and to lay out a series of grid lines. This was all ax work on snowshoes and was the first job that is required after the staking of claims. We would be living in tents, for the next six weeks, it was an exciting time. Before we left, we got our gear together, tents, sleeping bags, personal equipment, axes and everything else we thought we might need. The next step was to develop a plan showing the grid lines on paper and the starting points. The first job would be to establish the baseline then create the grid lines that would run at 90 degrees from the base. Future geological and geophysical work would be carried out using this grid. Information gathered in the field and plotted on the plan. Once our gear was together and the plans for the grid lines were developed, our instructor would go over everything to make sure that we had not missed anything.

With plans in place, the first loads of gear were hauled out to the site. Three tents two for sleeping and one for cooking. The location was about a mile off the road, and everything would have to be carried or pulled in on sleds. It took a couple of days to get the tents set up. There happened to be a tremendous amount of snow on the ground, and that made the setting of the tents a little more challenging. Buy the end of the second day the site looked perfect, clean, wood stacked, everything in order. Day three we came out with the full crew hiked in with our gear, foodstuffs, plans, and equipment required to do the job.

That morning on our first trip to our camp we could smell a campfire and see smoke off in the distance. Arriving at camp, we were greeted by a grizzled old mining veteran. Later we learned that this fellow was going to be our cook and supervisor when one of the other instructors were not there. He had coffee on, and it tasted damn fine. That trip we brought in the cooking supplies groceries and other odds and sods that were required to make our home away from home more comfortable. Had coffee, two guys stayed back and helped him set up the kitchen while the rest of us went back and got our personal gear sleeping bags, etc.

Dusk was coming fast, we had our sleeping bags, woods bags good for -40, all our own equipment stored. Now we're set ready to begin this adventure. Wood stoves in their tents going, portable lights, looked like a peaceful Christmas card from a distance, snowshoes all standing in the snow. Smoke billowing straight up a clanging noise disturbed the quiet, suppers ready. Off to the cook shack, we went. Everyone was famished. Supper completed corn beef hash tasted perfect everyone was starved. Setup cleaning schedule for dishes and other odds and sods in the kitchen. We all had our own coffee mugs, so that was one less thing for cleaning. This was an enjoyable evening on of many in the camp. Back to our tents we went, we could walk right in. But after six weeks and a multitude of snow storms, you barely see the opening, and the tents looked like snow caves, to get in it was like we were otter's and would slide down into the door and enter the tent. Snow was a fantastic insulator.

The next day we started our job. We had the plans showing the claims, the proposed grid layout, and the starting points. There was twelve of us. We started working on the baseline, and after two hundred feet, the first 90degree offset was set. One two-man crew went east while another two-man team went west. The remaining four teams continued to work on the baseline line until we had advanced another two hundred feet, then teams split off going east and west. We kept up this process for the day, by days end we had 2000 feet of the baseline cut, and the teams were working on the crosscuts. At lunch, each crew built a small fire for lunch, had toasted sandwichs it was easier to eat them that way warmed up for lunch. We would leave camp at daybreak and try and be back by dusk. We had six weeks to complete the job a formidable task. Day one done, just before nightfall, we all headed back to camp wondering, what would we have for an evening meal tonight.

Now the old veteran cook that we had was a great guy. The only thing, his cooking skills were somewhat suspect. As we headed to bed that first night after our meal of corned beef hash, some of the guys said did anyone else see how much, corned beef we brought to the kitchen today. We all laughed and said it will not be that bad. It did not take long, and we knew corned beef was here to stay. This was his main cooking ingredient; hell, I think back today it was his only ingredient. Corned beef the main staple in everything he cooked. In the morning eggs and maybe pancakes, with that, there would be corn beef hash. If we happened to be in camp at noon, it might be corned beef chili or leftover hash from breakfast or something along those lines. Thank god for lunches in the field, we had lunch meat, but when that was gone, then it was some kind of corned beef sandwich spread I fell in love with peanut butter, and jelly sandwiches as most of the crew did. Suppers where more of the same corned beef with onions, corned beef with cabbage always potatoes and rice. As far as meals went, we didn't die, and we survived to tell the story. After six weeks, they were 12 classmates who would never look at a can of corned beef the same way. To this day, I have never bought or opened canned corned beef again.

Life was good we got the job done on time, and it was a real learning experience. We completed our work, got together and started packing gear. The next morning, we would move out. Gear was packed, and we walked over to the cook shack for our last evening meal of corned beef. To our delight, there was no corned beef in site only steaks, and they were ready and waiting for us. A fitting end, a small celebration, of a job, well done. That night the guys in the other tent got there stove a little too hot and burnt their tent, just the front of it but it made for a chilly evening. They packed up their gear and moved into our shelter for the night. No one got hurt, and no personal equipment was lost. The crew felt sheepish for doing something so dumb.

Next day we packed the gear out and headed back to town.

Once we had written our reports on what we had accomplished for the last six weeks. The mining company accepted our work, the job was now 100% complete except for the final tear down and clean up. We traveled back and forth from the school to the site over the next three days. Hiked into the site knocked the tents down, packed the equipment out, cleaned up the place. All the remaining gear was loaded, and brought it all back to town, took a good week to sort dry and put everything away waiting for the next adventure, won't be me though, as our group was back to studying our core classes, waiting for the year to end.

That's It That's All

Grade twelve the final year, a good portion of the year consisted of NRT studies and travels. While the remaining part of the year was spent on core subjects.

When not out traveling or doing something with the NRT boys, there was plenty of time to spend with Carol. Spent many an evening with Carol, she would come over and help in the store. Other times we would go out on a date, mostly to the show or just go downtown for burgers and fries.

Christmas 69/70 Carol and I spent some of our time shopping for our family. Downtown, decorated, not much change from when I was a kid, it was always a magical time, music, lights, and Christmas smell's in the stores. We had a grand time that Christmas and spent every free moment we had with each other.

Christmas Eve Carol spent with her family. Went to midnight mass with Texaco Joe, we went up to the gallery, the plan was, as soon as communion was over, sneak out and head to Uncle Raymond's and Aunty Teresa's. This worked out well, we were sitting home, having a drink when the relatives, and mom and dad showed up. Of course, Aunty new we had snuck out before the end of the mass. She let us know that God was not going to be happy with us; we just laughed and continued having a good time. We had a lot of fun over the Christmas holidays but before we knew it, the holiday's were over.

I went back to high school, Carol back to college. Carol and I still saw each other, but when we went on our NRT mining job in February, Carol was meeting new friends, this was placing a strain on our relationship, just building blocks as we were in love. Through the year, we stuck together and did what we wanted to do. We enjoyed each other's company.

Spring of 1970 flashed by and before we knew it graduation time. High school was ending; my marks were between 65 and 70 not high, but good enough to be accepted at the college of applied arts and technology in Sault Ste. Marie. They had a geological program that was not offered in town so I would have to leave town to continue my education. My marks, well not good enough for university. First time I kicked myself in the ass, not hard though, I was still going to college, Dad and Mom were proud. I was extremely excited, I was going on to further my education.

I needed a job if I was going to go to school in the Sault in the fall. Dad and mom said they would help as much as they could, but I would have to work for the summer to earn some cash to help with the expenses. I found out that Falconbridge, a large mining company was looking for some summer students to do work on one of their properties northwest of Thunder Bay. This would be a fly in, fly out, job, cutting line and working with a geophysical crew. I was interested. Went to the interview, made a good impression, and got my first mining job. It would pay 335 dollars a month. I could hardly wait to get home and tell mom and dad, hopped on the bus, got back to the house and told them the good news.

They were happy and sad at the same time I was slowly leaving the roost. I informed Carol that night she was pleased, but let me know it was going to be a long summer as I would only be home a couple of times.

My high school graduation picture, we have come a long way.

The day came, graduation ceremonies, Carol looked gorgeous, I was decked out in a new suit, a special occasion, so we got to use dad's car. We set off for a night of pomp and fun. Twas a great night even though I had to have Carol home by midnight. Carols dad was an ass; we took what we could for time and enjoyed ourselves. Got Carol home, brought dads car back and waited for Ken to pick me up. Changed clothes into jeans, tee shirt, and cowboy boots and off to the races we went. One of our classmates was having a party at his parent's cottage not too far outside of Thunder Bay. The gathering was a bust, as it happened; just the NRT guys that showed up. Through the year we were the black sheep in school, not too many wanted to have anything to do with us. We sat around contemplated life. Here we were 12 of us that two years ago had no hope for an education, all of us graduated a remarkable feat. Talked about our two years together, remembering stories along the way, canoe trips, fishing, coffee, the American trip, the line cutting venture that only ended a few months back. The past was gone now what did the future hold, for me, off to college, continue with studies in geology and mining, I was going to be a miner of some sort, I felt it was my destiny.

Morning came we had breakfast, someone brought a couple of cans of corned beef, we looked at it and made a corned beef hash laughing the whole time. Not nearly as good, as what we had that first night a few months ago. I learned never to say never again because you never know what is around the corner. When we left the camp job that we had in the spring of 70, corned beef was never going to be on my menu for breakfast again.

Breakfast complete, my high school friends were leaving. Ken and I had become excellent friends. We looked around and left the cottage, closing the door on this aspect of our lives. This was the last time I saw any of them except for Ken. Ken and I stayed close for a long time. Then I decided it was time to start venturing out and seeing the country. We lost contact, and I made the fateful mistake of not staying in touch, later when I decided to look him up, it was too late, he had passed away in May of 2012.

Graduation was over, walked out of the cottage that morning, moving on to a new life. Started high school as a kid, full of wonderment, left as a man still looking for adventures but knew mining was going to be my ticket Looking back, I had an education; a wonderful girlfriend, life was grand, what a great time to start a new adventure.

Part 5
Out of the Nest

Falconbridge

Finished high school, I can say, done being a boy, now I am a man. In reality, I was still a boy, wet behind the ears.

After a week, it was time to start my summer job; Carol and I spent every waking minute together. Once I left, I knew it was going to be a long lonely summer.

I accepted a position working for Falconbridge Copper, Sturgeon Lake Joint Venture a subsidiary of Falconbridge Nickel. One of the premier mining companies of the day.

The day came when it was time to leave, gathered my gear, ax, rain gear, sleeping bag, and personal gear. We were to meet at the Falconbridge office. Dad gave me a ride; we had plenty of time to make it to the office. Dad taught me never keep others waiting, be on time or a bit early if you are first it never hurts anything. We arrived at the office, and I grabbed my pack and other gear, Dad looked at me and said, "Be careful, watch your step." I was only going away for the summer. As I look back, I was leaving home whether for a few days, or a week or longer I was starting to spread my wings, leaving the nest. I was going on my first adventure as a man. We hugged and repeated our goodbye's, and before I knew it, dad was gone.

Met the crew that I would be working with. The summer of 1970, a bush job, doing a geophysical survey on a block of claims northeast of Ignace Ontario. The camp was set up on Lyon Lake. No roads would have to fly in, another first.

With the paperwork complete. I was now an employee of Falconbridge Copper, (FC). Loaded a couple of small trucks and left Thunder Bay headed to Ignace, approximately three hours to the Northwest. Arrived stayed overnight at the Agimac hotel. Next morning we drove to Ignace Airways, located on Agimac Lake met our pilot, loaded the plane, a de Havilland Canada DHC – 2 beaver. This aircraft was a robust aircraft with short takeoff and landing capabilities. The primary aircraft used by the bush pilot of the day, to connect larger settlements with outposts in the bush, primarily moving men and materials.

With the plane loaded, men and gear, we headed out; the lake shimmered like glass on this quiet morning. I had the opportunity to be sitting up front beside the pilot. Another first in my short life. The plane made its way away from the dock, headed out into the bay and turned into the breeze. The pilot increased the power, and the airplane gathered speed as it came to life, before long we were hurtling down the lake. The power was unreal. As the pilot pulled the controls back the beaver lifted off the lake, we proceeded up into the blue sky. Before long the plane leveled out, we were heading northeast to Lyon Lake, about a 45-minute flight. I was mesmerized, this is great, an experience I would never forget. Looking out the window, I felt like an eagle soaring high, watching the trees and lakes slowly drift by. Before long, we passed over Flayers Lodge and Highway 599.

The pilot maneuvered the plane with great care, before long we started our descent, prepared for our landing on the lake. Seemed in a moment we touched down and made our way to the camp dock. As we were descending, I got a good view of the camp. Three tents set up in an excellent opening not too far from the lake.

We taxied to the dock and tied up; we unloaded our gear, the geophysical instruments, and the weekly grub order. Looking at the food order, I knew the meals here were going to be different, no cases of corned beef in sight.

As we were unloading, the plane an older man came to welcome us. He had a solid handshake, although he looked like he lived a tough life. His face showing a few days of growth, and his hair cropped short, a face so full of wrinkles it looked like a road map of the many years spent in prospecting. He bellowed out some orders, let us get this grub moved up to the cook tent, and then you can get your gear stored after that. As he walked away, he said supper will be at six o'clock and do not be late. This was the cook, a very gruff individual; I thought to myself, I sure hope he can cook.

Once we got the grub moved up to the cook tent, I noticed the other two shelters, this is where we would store our gear and place our weary heads after a long day in the field. Set my gear into one of the two tents. This tent had three cots, desk and a drafting table, and doubled as a field office as well as a bunk tent. Before long the party chief, the fellow who was in charge of the geophysical crew brought his gear into the tent. He would be staying with us. I knew I was going to learn a lot.

Once our equipment was stored, we moved outside to unpack that geophysical equipment. We laid the gear out on the ground, there were, ground probes, these were steel rods half an inch by two half feet long, rolls of wire, leads I learned that's what they were called, instruments, transmitters, recorders, batteries and an assortment of tools. The equipment, placed on select backpacks for carrying into the field. Our boss, the operator of the equipment set up some dry runs so we could learn what would be expected of us in the field. We packed all the gear, got it ready to move out. We would set out in the morning, to start the Induced Polarization Survey, (IP) for short.

The first couple of hours in the camp were busy. We found out that the plane would return once a week with grub and mail. If we had an emergency, there was a radio in the cook tent to contact the airbase in Ignace. This was going to be a great job, great camp, and one helluva summer.

Just relaxing in Camp.

Six o'clock arrived, and we moseyed over to the cook tent. This was going to be the first of many meals in this camp. Walking, into the cook-shack, what a

[231]

setup, tables, chairs a regular banquet hall in the bush. The first dinner in this elegant setup, chicken, potato, vegetables along with dessert, coffee, tea and Kool-Aid to satisfy our thirst.

Finished our meal, helped clean up, the cook told us, "leave it, I will do it," but one other fellow and I decided it was the least we could do. It was a great meal; this old man could really cook. No corned beef insight.

Back to the tent, the party chief asked me about my education; I explained just finished high school and graduated in Natural Resources Technology a program that provided me with some of the insights into mining. I would be attending college in the fall, taking a geological technician program. He asked me what I knew about geophysics. Told him just what I learned in school that it was a method of surveying the ground with electrical or magnetic measurements causing the earth to give up her secrets. The survey could find anomalies in the rock below the surface, and this could become targets for further exploration. We would start by laying the probes every 100 feet along a cut line, hook up the leads, proceed and add an electrical current. Through a series of calculations, the results then plotted on a plan, which could show anomalies beneath the surface. This was going to be an exciting summer and a summer of learning new things.

Dark outside now and time to shut down for the day. I stepped out of the tent to have a smoke. Looking up into the sky the stars where everywhere, sparkling like diamonds, felt like you could reach up and pluck them from their spot in the universe, put them in your pocket. Back into the tent, crawled into to my sleeping bag, I noticed how quiet it was, so quiet you could hear the garter snakes slithering after the mice in the tall grass. Before long, my eyes felt heavy and trying to close, sleep was getting ready to take over just as a loon let out a mournful, haunting sound, a sound that I would associate with my first summer in the bush, and a spot that I loved.

Next morning got up had breakfast eggs, bacon, sausage, and pancakes. I knew that we were not going to go hungry; again, this fellow proved to me, he knew how to cook. We made our own lunch and set off.

Brought all the gear down to the lake and loaded into canoes for a short trip across the lake to a small landing area. From here, we would walk into our work area. Once here, we started to lay out the gear as instructed. By noon, we are ready to put our IP survey at full speed. The rest of the day, we set out and moved the probes three or four times, took readings on each setup. My job was getting probes into the ground. Discussed with the operator to see if we could layout more than one set of probes at a time. Then we could just move the instruments hook up the leads and take the required readings. By the end of the day, we all knew what we were doing.

We headed back to camp and found that the cook would always have a big batch of Kool-Aid made up; we were thirsty when arrived back at camp. The problem was this was a small lake, and it was starting to warm up. We took the water directly from the lake, the water, good as it was, was not as tasty as we thought it should be. The second night had supper, let night settle in, called it an evening and slipped off to dreamland.

The job was going to be mundane, or so I thought. The next week everything was the same, up in the morning, breakfast, head out to the field, do IP surveys all day, back to the camp in the evening, shortly before six. We would have supper and back to our tent where we would work on calculations, using a slide rule, and then plot the results on the maps. The operator decided he would teach me how to do the calculations and plot the results upon the plans.

During the second week, the job was going well, we noticed in one area were getting erroneous readings. First, we thought the instruments were faulty, after some tests; the operator figured the equipment was fine. Then we thought we were not getting the probes into the ground right. That was not the problem. The operator figured the ground was too dry, so we started carrying water and dumping about 2 gallons on each probe just before we took the readings. This allowed for the better conductivity of the probes reaching the ground.
We always had lunch in the field, with a thermos of coffee or water from the many Cedar Swamp potholes, the water was sweet and cold better than the water that was coming from the lake. One day we got back to camp early so the operator could do a bunch of calculations to see if any sense could be made out of our erroneous readings.

A couple of other fellows and myself decided we would dig a well about 20 feet up from the beach. We had some lumber and timber we could use for cribbing. We proceeded to dig a hole about 10 feet deep, cribbed and then backfilled. In a couple of days the sands in the well completely settled out, and the water was clear and very fresh and sweet. Some of the guys decided to use the five-gallon bucket full of holes on the bottom, put their beer in the bucket and lower it into the well. Yes, back then, alcohol was allowed in camp, I do not remember any misbehaving though.

[234]

We could only get beer in if there was room on the plane.

When we got in from the field, we were very thirsty, and we would drink a lot because it was warm and we were dehydrated. The cook got a little angry with us though because we were filling up on Kool-Aid, juice, and water, then not eating supper and wanting something bigger than just a typical snack in the evening. The cook then decided that The Kool-Aid would not come out until supper was 3/4 done. That way, we were eating correctly and not just filling up on liquid.

After the fourth week, we were still getting erroneous readings. We did the perimeter of all the claims and plotted them on the plans. As we moved to the interior of the claims the readings were still off track. The operator decided we should take a couple of days off, go back to Thunder Bay and pick up some new instruments to see if we could alleviate this problem.

Being in camp for a month it was time for some R&R, we were going to get a few days off, time to fly out and head to Thunder Bay. We watched the plane come in, and it touched ever so lightly on the lake, then proceeded to taxi to the dock. We unloaded the grub brought it up to the cook tent, then loaded our gear and decided it was time to get out. The pilot guided the plane away from the dock, looked at a point down the lake that he was going to have maximum runway and revving engines until it felt like the tail was going to touch the water. Finally, we were moving forward, gliding down the lake at a tremendous speed, the plane started too gently lift into the air. It looked like we were going to head into the trees but we slowly climbed over the top, it felt like

[235]

I could reach out and touch the top of the trees as we went over the top. We made it into the air it was a great flight back to Ignace. A gentle landing, then the plane taxied to the dock tied up. We proceeded to unload our gear, jumped into the pickup and headed to Thunder Bay. We arrived at the office in the afternoon. Our boss told us to be at the office in two days at six AM, if we were not there, he would assume that we quit, and leave without us.

Called dad and he came and picked me up from the office. Got home cleaned up, jumped into the green beast, went and picked up Carol. She was amazed. We spent two days together even worked in the store for a bit, so the brothers could have a break. Being home was nice. The only thing about living with a group of people, in a camp, language becomes very blue at times; it just seemed to be the way of the bush. Many times, at the meal table, boys would be boys and the language used had a very blue tinge to it. Well at home, we were having supper, spaghetti, meatballs, Italian sausage, salad and fresh bread from Bennett's bakery. On the fresh bread, there was always a copious amount of butter used. Not even thinking I said "Brucey, please pass the f***ing butter," the words came out of my mouth, tongue engaged long before brain. I knew that I had crossed the line, dad looked at me, and I apologized for my language and said it would not happen again. Well, that was not good enough for the sergeant major I got dressed up and down; never again did I ever use that language in our house.

I had three weeks to complete my summer job, and then it was off to college. Back to the office, getting ready to leave. Our boss meant what he had said, one fellow was not there at six, and we left without him. The rule was if you wanted to work, you

[236]

were on time. Otherwise, you were left behind, and that is precisely what happened to this fellow.

We drove out and headed back to Ignace, our plane was scheduled to take off at 10:30 AM. As we drove back to Ignace, the operator and I were discussing how long it should take us to complete the survey. He said we should be done and 14 to 18 days, which will allow us, a couple extra days for checking areas that might need some additional work. Got to Ignace in plenty of time, loaded our gear and the new instruments onto the plane. We pulled away from the dock at 10:30 right on time. I was enjoying flying; it was peaceful and relaxing. Before long, we dropped out of the sky landed on the lake and taxied to the dock.

Unloaded the gear and the new instruments, changed into our bush gear and set out to do some tests with the latest equipment. We arrived at a site where we had good results with the old equipment and decided we would try the new equipment here. We proceeded to layout the probes and take measurements for the rest of the afternoon. Went back to camp calculated, and plotted the results. The results were the same as the old readings that we had taken two weeks ago. With that in mind, we headed out the next day to finish the IP survey.

The next day we moved into the area where we had erroneous readings. The new readings we were taking seemed to be correct as far as we could tell. The operator decided we would carry-on calculate and plot to see what would become of this Area. Over the next 16 days, all the areas were covered. The operator explained to me, he had never seen readings like this before, he felt there was definitely something there. We plotted the results on the plan, there was

[237]

definitely something different when you looked at the plot. A shape looked like the outline of a pear. Different readings on the outside vs. the inside. The operator explained to me that there are some definite drill targets here. The drilling he said should start in the center just to see what was causing the readings to be so erratic. He felt there was definitely some kind of ore here. The drilling, if it happens, would complete the exploration phase. I thought this was great, my first mining job, and possibly the uncovering of an ore body and a new mine in its infancy.

Time to call it a summer. The well we had dug really became a benefit to our camp life. I only had a couple of days left in camp. One of the guys from the line cutting crew decided to put some beer in the well to get cold. Proceeded to drop their beer into the well and all the bottles broke. We tested the water and had a horrible beer taste after that. The well was ruined, and we decided we had better backfill the hole, and pull the cribbing out. That was the last job we did in the camp. Also had heard that the camp was going to be moved closer to the claims so this area would become redundant. The plane showed we loaded up our gear took off made it out safely. Headed to Ignace great flight great adventure.

The plane landed safely, in Ignace offloaded the gear, then loaded it into trucks, and headed to Thunder Bay. I had $760 in the bank. Went home, cleaned up, and went shopping. Bought some new boots, a couple of pairs of pants, a couple of shirts and the bill was around $50. I thought that I was rich. After my shopping went and picked up Carol, had about a week left before I left for school in the Sault.

Carol was delighted to see me, and she had some news. She was moving out of her mom and dads, to an apartment on Arthur Street. Her landlady, an older widower, was very nosy. I helped her move, and one thing led to another. One day the landlady caught us in the hall and told us absolutely no shenanigans going on under her roof or Miss Carol you have to find another place to live. From then on, we were very quiet when coming and going.

The sergeant major made it known that she knew what was going on, told us it was OK, but be very careful so that we didn't get into something that we were not prepared for. The day was coming very quickly that I would be leaving, although Carol and I were still in love with each other, this newfound freedom of hers would cause a bit of a rift between us. We were talking a couple of days before I left and we were discussing whether we should be seeing other people while we were apart, the conversation went as well as could be expected, not good.

Dad and mom paid my tuition; I tried to get a student loan, no way. Dad and mom were making too much money, very different from when we were on the farm. I just had over $700 to last, and mom and dad said they would help in whatever way they could. I found two other people living in Thunder Bay that were taking courses at the college in Sault St. Marie. We could share travel expenses and an apartment together; my rent for a month would be $50. Carol and I went out that last evening, and then I dropped her off. Headed home, tears in my eyes, made it home packed my gear. In the AM, my ride showed up. Said goodbye to mom and dad jumped in with my partners and drove off.

First job-finished, high school finished, would the love of my life be there when I returned. Should have been a day of joy, it was a day of sadness; I left the nest sort of, my bed was still there and Ricky, Brucey, the Princess and the Prince still at home. Was coming to my 20th birthday and all I wanted was to go and start a new adventure. As we drove east, Nana Bijou the sleeping giant disappeared into the background along with two decades of my life. The giant was gone, I was sad and very quiet, all the wind taken out of my sails. Not sure, what the third decade would hold.

College

As I headed to college; was I prepared for this next adventure, would I be ready? Looking back now, I would say not. College was great; lots of fun, the geological courses were fantastic, core courses not so.

On my own, partying and school, not a good mix, the first month though I had a lot of fun. Was living up to my old standards, education, well if I get it, all is good, if not I was having a great time anyways.

Went home for the long Thanksgiving weekend. Would have to give mom and dad a report on how my marks were. Geology courses, high marks, remaining core courses, however, I was just passing, except for math, which was a fail. After reporting to mom and dad they both said I was going to have to pull up my socks and do better, they knew I had it in me. I had a great visit with mom and dad, and it is great to be home. I called Carol shortly after I arrived back to see if she wanted to go out and do something. She informed me that she already had other plans and that maybe I can call tomorrow and see what we can do. That night I decided to go out with Raymond's Joe. Things are going well for them, the garage and restaurant we are doing exceptionally well. After being away all summer and a couple months in the fall, I noticed it seemed like I was drifting away from family and friends.

Spent the next couple of days with Carol, but it was just not the same, seemed like there were defiantly cracks in our relationship.

I had Thanksgiving dinner with my family. Carol had Thanksgiving dinner with her family. The next day I left, headed back to the Sault, back to school never said goodbye to Carol, or her to me. Our relationship was drying up like a rose without water and sunshine. A curveball was thrown our way, there was a definite crack in our relationship. Not sure what the future will hold, next time I would be home would be Christmas, have to wait and see what that would bring.

School the next couple of months was a bust, marks dropped, doing reasonably well in the geological courses, but the core courses, however, were dismal, either just getting by, or failing.

When I first went down to the Sault, Carol and I would write almost every day, now towards getting close to Christmas, the letters were rare.

Had such a great time during the first four months. I really didn't pay any attention to my money. Needless to say, I was starting to run short I told mom and dad that I was going to need more, and they said they would help with what they could, but it's not going to be as easy as before. If my marks had been better, it would have been a different story. When I think back if I had paid more attention to school and less partying, probably would not have needed the money. In fact, dad told me that for the 2 to 3 weeks I was going to be home I should see if I could get a job to help make a little bit of extra money.

I got a hold of Falconbridge, just a check to see if they needed any help over the holidays. I was lucky; they did have work for me. I could go in and plot drill holes complete with results on the plans. These drill holes were from the Sturgeon Lake Joint Venture drill program. The IP survey showed promising areas and the next step in was drilling, and it moved ahead shortly after I had left the previous summer. I was curious to see what kind of results that the drilling showed.

I made it home for the holidays, I would have to say it was great being with family, Carol and I parted ways on our first night out, I was devastated.

Work started the next day; not allowed to talk to anyone outside of the office about this project. Overlooking the plan, I plotted the exploratory hole, the first drill hole. It was what the IP operator had suggested a massive sulfide deposit. I started plotting other holes. The results were fantastic; they showed high-grade copper, lead and zinc with tremendous values of silver associated with the ore body. I was looking at a new mine in its infancy.

The manager told me that I should take my money and buy shares; as soon as the results are made public, the share value would take off. They were trading at about $1.25 per share. The results would be made public, in mid-January. Told him I could not do it as I needed the money for school Uncle Nic, had taught me that the stock market was not a sure thing?

I went home and told dad, he decided to pass saying he figured he could get a better value on the crap table.

Christmas came, did some Christmas shopping no magic this year. Went to midnight mass with all relates that part was grand. Christmas this year held no charm for me. I was working downtown so I could see all the lights and listen to the music when I was waiting for the bus. It just seemed like noise. The magic I remembered as a kid or even a couple of years back was gone. Would it be found again?

Carol was visiting her mom and dad over the holidays at home and stopped at the store, I was not there, I went out with Ken, I had not seen him since the summer. She told my brother, could you ask Joe to give me a call, I got a message decided I would just pop in and see her. The joke was on me, she was coming out the door as I was knocking, could not talk now, as she was going out with this other fellow. A friend from college I gathered. She said that maybe we could get together tomorrow. I said thanks but no thanks; I was busy, even though I was not. In three days, it would be time to head back to the Sault and return to school. Finished my job, said goodbye to mom, dad, brothers, and sister. Left and headed out, did not inform Carol or see her again our love was over as far as I was concerned. We would go our own separate ways.

I had to be careful with my money; the partying was not as prevalent as before. Hindsight is lovely, the shares in Falconbridge Copper came on the stock market in mid-January, and the opening price was 4 times greater than I could have purchased them. If I had bought and sold, I would have had plenty of cash to finish my first year of college. Not having the cash was a good thing, struggling for money kept me grounded. In fact, I gathered up all the empty bottles and took them back to the LBCO. Used the money to by some groceries, bologna and bread, no corned beef but after a month the bologna was moving into the same category. Mom and dad came through, and I got enough money to finish the year. A good lesson, learned, party hard, and you will starve, and your marks will suffer.

Started dating some other girls, was fun but just not the same. Going to dances at the college did some bowling it was cheap entertainment. After a couple months, my marks, coming back. My geology subjects were still great, and the core subjects showed a remarkable improvement, I was passing everything. I decided to write Carol, just to see how she was doing. Low and behold came back from school one day and there was a letter from her, something I did not expect, she wrote back. We continued writing found out she was not going with anyone, asked why, and she told me, it did not work out, not as much fun as I thought it was going to be. I offered sincere regrets and told her to keep looking it will get better. She was working a new job now, working for a construction company in Thunder Bay North not too far from her apartment. I kept our conversations general, as I was hurt once and I figured she was just looking for a friend. Life was good, marks were improving, and I had a new group of friends nothing permanent, just good friends. Carol, seemed happy about that.

At the beginning of April, I got a letter from Carol, and she said she would like to come for a visit. I thought it was an April fool's joke.

I wrote back, said sure. In a couple weeks, I met Carol at the Greyhound station. She looked fantastic when she got off the bus. I took her to a motel that was only a couple blocks away from my apartment. There was not enough room at my place, as I was sharing with two other guys.

That night we went to college dance, I introduced her to many of my friends. By the end of the night, she had moved very close, anytime one of my friends stepped in and asked for a dance, she became very possessive.

The last dance came, back in the day, the final dance it was always something you could slow dance to, we moved slowly around the dance floor, she whispered in my ear, apologizes for all the pain she had caused me.

After the dance, we walked back to the motel where she was staying. On the way, I asked her what she wanted if this was going to be just another game until someone better came along. She stopped looked into my eyes and said no, that she loved me.

It was hard for me to understand, I did not know where we would end up. My gut was telling me, that I still had strong feelings for Carol, where we were going; I was always in love with her. We got to the motel, made sure she was safe, and I said that I had better get going. She asked me "aren't you going to come in"; I said, "No, I wanted to think things through." I left and proceeded to walk home. It was a hard walk. The next morning I picked her up for breakfast, and then we went out. Toured the locks and did a few touristy things. That evening went out for supper then went bowling. Walked her back to her motel room again she asked, "Are you going to come in," I said "are you sure you want to do this," she said "yes." The door closed, I held her in my arms and told her how much I loved her.

Next morning, it was our last day together; she had to head back to Thunder Bay. We wandered around town, went for lunch and supper and back to the motel room we are sitting on the bed, I looked her square in the eyes, and I asked her again "are you sure you want to do this," and she answered, "yes I love you." I kept looking at her and said: "would you marry me." "Yes," she replied a paperclip bent in a circle, used to seal the deal. We decided we would keep it to ourselves until I could get her a real ring. Next morning, I saw Carol off at the bus station, watched her leave, I was on cloud nine, she seemed to float in the air.

The remaining part of the year passed quickly, worked hard brought my marks up to a semblance of normal. Had one more year at college to go, this year was over now. Had two job offers for the summer, one in Sudbury at the Inco Nickel operations and one back in Thunder Bay for Falconbridge.

Summer of 1971

College out traveled to Sudbury, decided to take the summer job with Inco. The hiring process was quite an ordeal. First spent the day filling out paperwork, next day was for medicals. This was like joining the forces 20 or so students all in a line dressed only in their skivvies. A couple of doctors moving up and down the line looking at you, probing, and prodding had to be sure you were qualified and fit for work. This process took the better part of a day. The job Inco was offering was to be an underground laborer. Started thinking, is this really what I want. I phoned the manager at Falconbridge in Thunder Bay at lunch, he still had a position open. Would be cutting line surveying, marking out drill sites, tent living, but a bigger camp. Pay would be in the neighborhood of $500 per month. The pay differential going underground and surface would be about $50 per month. But staying in Sudbury, I would have to rent a place for the summer buy food and be away from Carol. If I went back to Thunder Bay, I would be closer to Carol, room, and board supplied by Falconbridge, on days off, have a place to stay, mom and dads. Standing back in line after lunch and being poked one last time I thought, nope I am out here, I want to be closer to Carol and look at the stars at night. Told Inco thanks for the opportunity, caught the next bus and headed home.

When down to the Falconbridge office, signed up, found out the job would last until mid-August. Moved out to camp as quick as I could, needed the money because I wanted to buy an engagement ring for Carol. The job was exciting, and I was working with a great bunch of people. Robert Patterson and Ron Gashinski took me under their wing. Here I was, back on this site, where I was a year ago. The job entailed surveying, cutting line, marking out diamond drill holes. The property had the makings of becoming a mine, it was exciting. I was hooked on mining, embarking on a new career, along with getting married to my sweetheart.

Halfway through the summer, Carol came up for a visit, and we stayed at Flayers Lodge just outside of Ignace north on Highway 599. Falconbridge let me use a truck for the weekend, and we had a fabulous time. We started planning the wedding; we decided on November 27, 10 days after Carol's 20th birthday and the same day Nana and Papu were married so many years ago. She went back home to Thunder Bay, and I went back to camp continued working on the odd jobs until complete, it was mid-August, and it was time to go back to Thunder Bay.

Got back to Thunder Bay, went out and bought Carol an engagement ring, it was white gold, small diamond but the setting made the diamond look bigger. We purchased, and old rambler car that would be our primary means of transportation, kind of dusty rose in color with fold-down front seats. You could lay right down it was like a bed. My cousin Frank called it a shagging wagon. It really was a cool car.

We went out one afternoon, stopped at the Dairy Queen, went and got us a couple small ice cream cones. I spoke to the concession girl and told her what my plan was she went along with it and we buried the ring in her cone about a quarter of the way down. Paid for the cones and brought them out to the car, we were sitting there eating our ice cream discussing what would we do with our lives. Decided I was not going back to school in the fall. I would get a job somewhere and continue working until we

[249]

became established; I thought to myself that this would put my mining career on hold. She was slowly licking the cone when all of a sudden there was a shriek, what is this she demanded to know. Pulled it out, and her eyes filled with tears, I took the ring cleaned it off and slipped it on her finger, and made it formal "will you marry me" and she replied "yes." We finished our cones and went to see mom and dad, show them the ring and tell him the date we had picked. They were happy. From here we went to Carol's parent's house, Carol's mother, her brother, and sister were delighted her dad not at all, but we did not expect anything different. Nevertheless, he made it known to us do not expect anything from us we are not giving a nickel towards this relationship. Carol and I left, and Carol was in tears, I told her do not worry we will make it work. Went back to mom and dads, we decided to work in the store for a while and give the kids a break that way Carol and I could discuss the wedding plans without interruption.

While we were in the store, a man came in. He was a long-time customer and worked for a construction company, Barbini Construction, building apartments, schools, office buildings as well as brick facings on houses, using precast concrete, concrete blocks and bricks.

"I see you're back now," he said while standing in the store, I said "yes," and he asked me if my job in the bush was finished, I replied, "Yes it was." Joe are you looking for work. I said "yes." We are hiring some laborers for an apartment build over on Hudson Avenue are you interested. I replied, "Yes I sure am." "Good, I will meet you there on Monday morning to get you started." Great, new job, things are looking up already. Left Carol in the store went back and told mom and dad the great news. Mom and dad were

[250]

happy. Back to the store, Carol and I started planning our wedding with a new sense of urgency. It would be a small affair with no more than 150 people, unlike most of the Italian celebrations of the day 300 to 500 guests. With a little wedding and a new job, it meant that we would be able to pay for the hall the meals and drinks. The venue not decided upon yet but knew we were moving in the right direction.

Our marriage would take me in a different direction; gone would be the adventures for a while. I would be working in Thunder Bay no glamorous jobs in the field. Mining sitting on the backburner for now. I had to work, stay home and support my family. Life, another curveball, mining on the back burner, with construction moving to the front and in which direction are we heading not 100% sure. Thought about those days in high school when I turned up my nose at the blue-collar jobs and staying in Thunder Bay. It seemed so long ago.

Our Start

I was 20, Carol was 19, and we were embarking on a life journey that no one knew how it would end. We both thought we would be together, for an eternity that was our plan.

The Christmas of 1968, I met Carol, and now here we are almost three years later going to get married. Mom and dad, and Carol's mom were happy, her dad definitely not.

The grandparents on all sides had different reactions. Nana and Grandma Estrid were fine with it. Carols grandparents on her mom's side wished us a life full of love and happiness. Carols dads parents were the complete opposite. Happiness, there was none here. Carol was an Anglican, and I was Roman Catholic. Her grandma and grandpa made it known that she was marrying a dogan, Carol told them that I was not Irish, I was Italian, that made matters worse, their thought, she was marrying a criminal, all Italians are criminals. I was not sure how I was going to get them on our side, my side then I thought who cares what they think I am not marrying them I am marrying Carol. The next few months they kept telling Carol I was a mistake, he is just not right for our family. You have to put a stop to this nonsense. These conversations carried on right up to the night before the wedding. This nonsense has to stop. Carol would have nothing to do with their conversations. Each day the storm would come, and each day it would pass. They let it be known that they could not possibly attend this get-together; I was hoping cooler heads would prevail, as the time got closer. Carol and I just looked at each other and realized we had a big day to plan, our forever day.

We looked at each other and laughed where do we start? We grabbed a piece of paper and proceeded to develop a plan. We marked down jobs to be completed and jobs that were complete. Have we accomplished anything yet? Dad always said have a plan.

Our Plan

- Date of the wedding: November 27, 1971
- Where: Thunder Bay, Ontario
- Size of wedding small no more than hundred people, including Family and friends.
- Who would be maid of honor, bridesmaids, flower girl/ ring bearer?
- Who would be Best man, groomsmen?
- Gowns and dresses, Tuxedos or suites
- Flowers
- Invitations
- Pictures
- Gifts for bride and groom
- Wedding rings
- Church or justice
- Venue for reception

After about an hour we knew we had our work cut out for us, so far we decided yes were getting married and on what date.

The first thing we decided it would be a church wedding in Saint Anthony's parish, on banning street, this was the church of my family and being Roman Catholic, this was the one thing we couldn't get away from. We made an appointment with the priest the Reverend Micheal J O'Brien, a fairly progressive priest at the time, to go and discuss our plans. The first hurdle, the church at the time we picked would be going through a retrofit, and it would not be complete for our big day, will that be a problem. We looked at each other and said no, our life is a construction project anyways always tinkering and building to make it better. The second hurdle Carol was an Anglican, Father O'Brien told us we would have to take classes in the Roman Catholic teachings. I asked why and does this mean that Carol will have to convert to Catholicism, Father O'Brien explained no that would not be the case as Anglicans were very close to the Catholic religion it was more to make sure what was expected from us in the future, our relationship with the church, kids, etc. We said okay, and our classes were set up we had 5 classes, then we would write a simple test and then that would satisfy the church. Carol explained this to her mother, she didn't have any problem but her dad and grandparents, just another nail in my coffin as far as they were concerned, they wanted Carol to quit this nonsense before it's too late. We finished our classes and wrote our tests and that part of the checklist was completed, we would be married November 27, 1971, at 3:00PM in Saint Anthonys Parish with Reverend Micheal J O'Brien officiating.

Next thing on our list was picking our bridal group. Carol was working at headway corporation at the time and became very good friend's with a young woman by the name of Roberta Love, a single mom. She had a little girl that Carol had fallen in love with her name was Laura Kimbers. Carol asked Roberta to be her Matron of Honour and Laura was going to be the flower girl. The princess as she was so fondly called, Charlotte my sister and a good friend of Carol's, Bernice Hermanson from high school were bridesmaids, this rounded out Carol's bridal party. They got together and decided on gowns and the color

[254]

scheme for the wedding. Red and white gowns the red was the color of sweetheart roses. At this time Carol ordered her gown, $105.00 probably the most expensive single item for the wedding. A $10.00 deposit was required.

On my side, it was a lot easier, we would rent tuxedos from Hymers men's ware. A neighbor from just down the street. He always came into our store and gave us what business he could, now was the time to reciprocate.

Ricky was my best man, Brucey, and Raymonds Joe was now known as Texico Joe because they were selling Texico gas at the garage, were my groomsman. The little prince, could not forget him was asked to be the ring bearer. That rounded out my side of the bridal party, the plan was moving along nicely. One more item checked off the list.

As we were checking jobs off our list, we realized that we were going to need a place to live. We had to find a place to live. We were not going to live with Carol's mom and dad, and there was not enough room at my parent's place. So we needed to find a place that we could call our own. That's what we really wanted anyway, the parent option was not really an option. We were working and planning the wedding we decided to search for an apartment for the two of us. We searched high and low. We found a place, 27 Shuniah Street this would be where we would rest our weary heads after a hard day of work. It was a two-bedroom second story apartment, and the rent was reasonable, $100 a month. It needed a paint job so if we bought the paint and did the work ourselves he would give us our first three months at 75.00 per month. So we accepted, and the apartment was ours starting on October 1st. We spent the next two months painting and cleaning and getting

[255]

furniture moved in, making sure that our place would be ready for us to move into when we became man and wife.

Purchasing invitations, this job had to be completed rather quickly so we could send them out and get a count of the number of people that would be attending the reception. Along with ordering the invitations, we had to come up with a list of people we would invite. Carol settled on the invitation it was elegant and stylish. To this day some 45 plus years later I think they still look great. We completed the list of invitees. I gave my input another job well done.

As we were looking at the invitations, we realized we needed to find a venue and a band for the reception. The Italian hall was interested, but even with dad being a member it was going to be expensive because of the size of our reception small. Dad came to the rescue on this, he said: " you know Uncle Nickey, and Uncle Johnny, are opening a high-end Italian Supper club, you should talk to them, maybe they would be interested." Carol and I thought this might be a good idea. So we set up a meeting, found out they were going to have their grand opening on the second weekend of October just after my twenty-first birthday. We explained our plan, and they said they would be happy to host the reception, so we set up the menu, not too hard; standard fare for an Italian celebration. The club would have to be shut down as this would be a private affair. The price we received for using the club, the meals, and drinks, for 100 guests was in the range of 600 to 800 dollars. Carol and I agreed, shook hands, payment to be later, it was family, another box checked off our list.

That same day we went to Vals Card and Party Shop and completed the order for the invitations and party favors. The invitations and the rsvp's came to

$53.00 while the favors, napkins, and matches came to $23.00, a total of $76.00, had to put a deposit down of $5.00, times were simple then.

October was flying by, my twenty-first birthday came and went. Carol and I went to Tinos to celebrate, more as a check to satisfy our own curiosity that we had made the right decision on using Tinos for our reception. By the end of the night, any fears that we had were set aside it was a wonderful evening.

November rolled around. Bought our wedding bands a total of $35.00 my gift for Carol, a charm bracelet, and charm $35.00, Carol's gift for me gold chain was $15.00. Ordered the flowers bouquets and boutonnieres, $95.00, found a photographer for our big day $60.00. A week before, we were ready, the wedding would cost around $1500.00, close $10,000 in 2017 dollars. We were ready.

During the two weeks, before the wedding Carol had a few showers to attended to, Rick and dad decided we would have a stag party, to be held in the basement at Uncle Raymond's house on John Street. It was a big basement could hold a lot of people, set up well, we had drinks, food, and games of chance. Was kind of neat, each game table set aside around 5% of each winning pot, this went into the groom's pot, a pot of money that would be given to the groom at the end of the evening. This would help with the startup costs of our new venture. I had my allowance for the evening around, $40.00 was learning how to play craps and found this was not the game for me. Before I knew it, I had $10.00 left put that in my pocket. It was time to become a social butterfly, had drinks with the invited guests and told stories, and lots of BS was passed around. Buy the end of the night I was lead home, thrown into the bedroom, woke up the next morning green around the gills, but I still had my $10.00 in my pocket only down $30.00. That evening Carol and I got an envelope from dad containing just over $200, our cut from the proceedings from the night before.

Construction Work A New Start.

We both had jobs, to keep us occupied. I was working for Barbini construction as a general laborer. During this time, I was learning a multitude of different tasks. How to set and tie rebar, set and erect scaffolding, the in's, and outs of laying blocks and bricks as well as what the bricklayers required to make the job run smoothly. I learned how to mix mortar; this job was usually relegated to someone with whiskers. Someone who knew how much water, cement, and sand would be required to make a good bonding material.

I was making just over five dollars an hour. It was a great job, hard work but the pay was damn good. Each Friday, the paymaster, would come to the job site we were working on. He would then proceed to give us our pay envelopes. Cash money for the previous week's work. The only problem with this system, it was too easy to spend. One had to learn monetary discipline in a hurry, or you would be broke in no time flat.

While working for Barbini, I had to join the union, The International Brotherhood of Labourers. Not sure how this was going to work out, but it was a requirement for the job. As a group, the union had a lot of power in the construction industry. They represented us; they would do all of the negotiations for the group, wages, benefits, overtime were all factors that were being dealt with. The union, of course, always blew their own horns as to how important they were. The union informed us that without them the company would screw us. We will lose wages, benefits and our rights to eke out a normal living. During this time, the union was

[259]

negotiating a new contract a two-year deal with some wages and benefits increases. The union called a meeting, and I was required to attend to discuss how negations were moving along. I talked to dad, and as an old union member, he told me I should go to the meeting just to learn about what was happening what the union is trying to achieve for us. I decided it would not hurt, so I went.

I walked into the hall there was a large group of men attending, this meeting. A league of all nations. Union leadership sat at the front, and it was their job to explain to us how the negotiations were progressing over the last couple of months. I found out that at the beginning of negotiations there were some lofty expectations, a minimal increase of 10% in wages, better benefits and better vacation package. No one took a vacation in the summer as this was the prime construction season; everyone saved vacation time for the offseason construction period in the winter months.

As we found out negotiations were not going very well no increase in benefits no increase in vacation time and a paltry 1% increase in pay.

The men listened to this update, and one could feel the tension in the room was building. As each man spoke, anger was becoming more prevalent. The leadership was telling us, listen to us we know what we are doing. I found out in a hurry these people were politicians with a different stripe, telling us to vote for them, we know what you need and what is best for you. A quick scan of the room showed that the room was split down the middle, half of the men wanting to go on strike immediately, and half-saying stay on the job. The half that said we should stay on the job now made a lot of sense. Soon the construction industry would slow down for winter, and the layoffs will start. Walking off the job now will not have the desired effect on the companies; the season was drawing to a close. We all have bills to pay, and we can't afford a strike right now. I thought to myself, I have only been working in this industry for a month now, I need a paying job, and strike pay will do me no good. I had a wedding to pay for in a couple of months, I need all the work I can get. Before I knew it, the lines were drawn, and many angry words were being bantered about. I started moving to the back of the hall, and I was going to sneak out of this mess. Got to the doors and they were closed and being guarded by a couple of union executive members. They knew what I had in mind, told me to sit down and listen no one was leaving until this matter was resolved. I took a chair at the back of the hall and watched the proceedings unfold before my very eyes. A fellow is speaking, about the advantages of continuing to work while negotiations were ongoing. All of a sudden, another man got up, tapped this person on the shoulder and before I knew it, he threw a punch. All hell broke loose. Chairs crashing, bodies rolling, and words in a multitude of languages being yelled. The shenanigans when on for about 15 minutes until everyone calmed down and the meeting was brought back to order. A vote had been called, and it was decided to continue to negotiate in good faith. The meeting was adjourned I got out of there in a hurry and went home. Told dad about the meeting and he chuckled. This is my first union meeting and my last. I paid my dues but never went back to any more union meetings. Mined my own business and worked on my work ethic. When negations were complete, we got a 2% wage increase some minor benefits, and Saturday a new rate pay would be time and a half.

It seemed that working overtime on Saturdays for the company was a moot point, it never happened. Saturdays were the days that the bricklayers did small jobs around the city. The jobs would include bricking houses, landscaping, jobs that were too small for the company to be involved in. Supplies purchased through the company so, in essence, they did get a cut of the work. Good work paid well. I would take as many jobs as I could get. This was cash money, and the more you worked, the more you were paid.

About a week before the wedding, the construction industry was entering its winter shutdown period, and I received a layoff notice. Thought to myself now what two salaries to one, from $300 a week down to $100 a week, Carol and I decided that I would look for a new job after the wedding.

Our new landlord was a window installer. He heard that I had been laid off and he asked if I would be interested in helping him on a project that would last another six weeks, right up until Christmas. I said sure. Working again, a short-term job would help pay the bills. I started thinking is this what it is going to be like for the rest of my life. Continually searching for a job, working, laid off, find a new job, and work again. Embarking on a construction career might have its advantages for the short term, it paid the bills. Long term not sure.

Our Day

Friday, November 26, arrived like any other day. Woke up in the morning got up chatting with mom and dad. Sitting there having coffee, the last day of being single.

Reminiscing, gone were the days of that little boy wandering the streets of little Italy. The days on the farm disappeared like the water in the creek. Six years ago, we opened the store now it was time to leave, cross over to a time of uncertainty, but be sure it was a time filled with love. A day filled with sadness and happiness. Gone were the days of innocence and childhood. A young man now, moving on to adulthood, turned 21 with a full-time job. Thinking to myself, I am going to start a new adventure, with a new partner.

The last day being single moved rather quickly. Some last-minute touch-ups to get ready for the big day. All the boys went downtown and picked up their Tuxedo's, I picked up Carol's wedding gift and the flowers that were required for the groom's party. Carol spent her day running around with her bridesmaid picking up the remaining flowers and any other trappings that were required for the bride's party. Carol's mom was finishing up the wedding cake a four-tiered dark fruit cake with almond paste icing. Before we knew it the day was over, Carol spent her last single night at home with her parents and her grandparents. Rumor has it that her dad and her grandparents tried everything possible to dissuade her from going through with the wedding. To no avail, she would have none of it. The girls in her party would meet at her parent's house to get ready. A compromise had been reached, her dad would give her away, her parents, grandparents on her dad's side would attend the nuptials in the church, along with her brother and sister but they were not going to attend the reception. Her mom's parents were living in Edmonton and could not make it to the wedding, but sent a cheque to help us out as well as a wonderful letter wishing us a lifetime full of health and happiness.

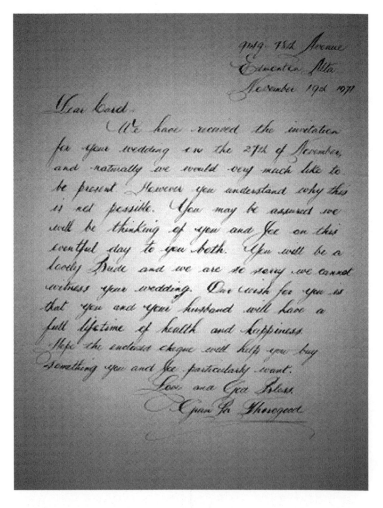

Letter from Carols Grandparents in Edmonton.

That evening I went and visited Aunty Teresa for any words of wisdom, be good, be true, is all she told me. We sat around in the basement Texaco Joe, Ricky and Cousin Frank, Brucey and Leonard were out cruising around town. Spent the better part of the evening here, shared stories talked about life in general. Then the evening was over went home crawled into bed, the last night sharing a bedroom with brothers, tomorrow night will have a new partner sharing my bed, smiled and drifted off to sleep.

November 27th arrived. Opened my eyes, moseyed upstairs, had a wonderful breakfast of eggs and Italian sausage, everyone was bustling all around, Brucey, Ricky, and dad taking turns in the store. The sergeant major barking out orders so everyone knew where they stood, we were not going to be late, and this wedding was going to go off like clockwork. Mom Said "Joey go and change and get ready," "mom it's only 10:00 we got lots of time" I replied, I figured might as well go and start to get ready just to keep the peace for the day. The store was open until 1 PM then shut down for the rest of the day. Everyone was ready, by 2:00 PM we headed to the church. Dad, mom, the groom's party, and of course a little prince made our way inside the church. Watching the little prince was rather funny, there he was all decked out in his Tuxedo, you would've thought that this was his special day. He was prancing around like a peacock.

The proud Prince

As we walked into the church, I looked around, Father O'Brien was right yes, it was under construction, and the Reno's were coming along quite well. The church had no resemblance to what I remembered from all the times I was in here. It did look quite different drywall and drywall tape all over, it did not matter it was only a building, the words that were to be spoken would come from our hearts filled with love. People started to gather, and the pews were being filled; Brucey and Texaco Joe were seating people. Dad and mom were sitting in the front pew along with Nana and Grandma Estrid; as I sit here thinking back to that day, this was a day when my family was all-together for something great. The only ones that were missing were, Papu and Grandpapa, I knew they were watching from heaven I could feel the warmth. My godparents Aunty Teresa and Uncle Raymond were there beside mom and dad like they were so many years ago on their big day. The rest of the family aunts, uncles, cousins from both sides rounded out participants from my side of the family.

Ricky and I were in the rectory, talking just passing the time. Father O'Brien stopped and asked if we were ready, looked at him and smiled. There was a commotion outside. Ricky peaked out and said do not worry the bride has arrived. Ricky looked at me and said, "Ready to go" I replied, "I think so" he looked at me and said, "do not think just do it." So we moseyed out to the front of the church, there were many people there all with smiles and tears. I looked over and saw Carol's mom and her grandparents, along with her brother and sister sitting, her mom and brother and sister were smiling. Her grandparents, on the other hand, looked like something right out of a horror movie. Her grandfather looked like he was hung over and wanted to be anywhere but here. I looked directly at her grandmother, the look I got could cause paint to crack or water to freeze over. I knew if Carol saw this it would upset her, and possibly ruin our day. I looked at Rick, and he knew what I was about to do. I slowly walked over in front of her bent down and whispered in her grandmother's ear. I know you do not like me, but I do not care. The least you could do is put a smile on the old face of yours. If not for us at least for your granddaughter. It will not crack I will guarantee it. Then went back and stood beside Rick, Rick gave me the look of approval, as I glanced over my shoulder at Carol's grandmothers face, she had a look of astonishment about her, she could not believe what had happened.

Carols Dad walking her down the aisle

Standing in the front of the church waiting nervously, but excited at the same time. The music started, and I looked towards the entrance of the church. The groomsmen and bridesmaids appeared, and the procession had started. All heads turned, watching and waiting for the bride to appear, and then the maid of honor was next, walked down the aisle and took her position by the altar. I watched and waited, anticipating who would be next. The flower girl and ring bearer started to make their way down the aisle. The applause started to happen, she was moving down the aisle holding on to her dad's arm, he was smiling, I glanced over at Carols mom and grandparent's they were all smiling. I stood there watching her make her way to the front of the church.

I was nervous, excited and proud as my body shook with happiness and a tear rolled down my cheek.

We locked eyes, and the message was clear, I love you, I love you back. Carol took her place at the altar, and father O'Brian asked who gives this woman to be married to this man. Carols father answered with a smile "I do." This was the start of the wedding, about 45 minutes later after exchanging our vows we were pronounced man and wife. I kissed my bride and held her quietly in my arms as tears rolled down my face; I would say I was the happiest man in the world at that particular moment. We walked down the aisle together Carol's arm locked in mine with smiles on our face that would light up a cloudy day. Coming out of the church dad was one of the first to give Carol a hug and welcome her to the family, after months of preparation we were outside the church shaking hands, receiving hugs and well wishes from our family and friends.

Joe and Carol at the alter
[269]

*The church was definitely under construction I was
oblivious to it all*

*In as two single entities out as Mr. and Mrs. Joe
Agostino*

The reception was set for 6 PM, so we left the church, went for a quick spin around town then off to the photographers to have some photographs taken to mark this day in eternity. Mom and Dad went home for a bit, so did Carol's mom and dad, we stopped at Carol's place for a bit, and I asked if maybe they changed their mind about the reception no such luck although Carols brother and sister would be there a small victory. I felt for Carol squeezed her hand so she would know it would work out. We left there went to my mom and dads stopped had a quick drink a shot of rye a tradition for special occasions that I grew up with.

We left the house and proceeded to the reception. We arrived around 5:30PM, a bit early we thought. The little prince took it upon himself that he was going to help Carol out of the car. She needed help with her train, he thought he should be the one to help. This didn't quite work out as well as expected. I really do not know what happened, but as she was stepping out she fell into my arms, the little prince tugged and pulled on the train then let go, out Carol spilled. I was about to tear a strip off him, and Carol stepped in, and in a quiet voice explained that she would take care of the train and she would like it if he just walked beside her. All was at peace; the prince was beaming from ear to ear so was I. Carol's dad dropped Carol's brother and sister off at the reception, they were ecstatic that they were there. Many years later rumor had it that, that night Carol's mom and dad, and grandparents had ordered a meal while we were dining on an exquisite Italian feast. They ordered takeout from the Italian Hall, spaghetti, and meatballs. Carols grandparents were not happy with this; I thought it was a fitting end to their day.

[271]

Tino's Restaurant and Supper club, not a bad place considering it was once a grocery store

We entered Tino's the place was magical; Uncle Nick and Uncle John did a fantastic job. There were people inside waiting for us to make an appearance. The evening went like clockwork. The meal was fantastic enjoyed by all, the Hi-Lites the same band that played for Tino's grand opening played at our wedding, of course, they were all relates cousins and such; we danced and kissed the night away. We snuck out, went to the hotel room that we had booked earlier, and Carol changed from her gown into something more casual. Proceeded to go back to the reception. Around 11 PM, we threw the garter, and some poor soul gathered it in hoping it would bring some magical moments to their own lives.

It was time to cut the cake then move around pass the cake out as we thanked everyone for coming. The cake well it was only a three-tier cake, not the four-tier that I was expecting. I looked at Carol, and she said that she would explain later what happened to the fourth tier. I never did find out what happened, but rumor has it, that the fourth tier had been destroyed the night before the wedding in a food fight. Carols mom proceeded to hide the remaining parts of the cake; this cake had a special meaning for both of us. I did not realize how much animosity there was between Carol's dad and her grandparents about our wedding. As far as I was concerned, it was their loss. I knew that night that Carol not having her mom and dad at the reception hurt her. Dad knew what was going on and became a lifetime friend of Carols.

The wedding cake made it minus one tier

Our first dance as a married couple

Wedding group photo

Family Photo, Dad, the Prince, Mom, the Princess
Rick Left, "Tony's Joe" middle Bruce on the right.

Carols brother and sister, Murray on the left, Heather
on the right

Joe and Carol Agostino "Tony's Joe" has left the nest

We passed out the cake and between handshakes, hugs, and kisses we made it around, saw, and thanked everyone. We received a pile of good wishes, and we decided it was time to have one last dance, sneak off and start our new life.

We snuck off to our hotel room for the night; our first night spent at the Prince Arthur Hotel a magical place of the day. We sat in our room on the bed opening gift cards, we stopped and looked at each other not saying a word but reading each other eyes, welcome to the rest of my life, I love you. We kissed and hugged turned out the lights. Holding each other close, man what a journey. I held her tight never wanting to let go, as I drifted off to sleep what would the morning bring as we were embarking on a new journey together.

Made in the
USA
Columbia, SC